the

FAR

and the

NEAR

David Lehner

D1411463

Peace, peace, to the far and the near, saith the Lord,

and I will heal them.

But the wicked are like the tossing sea that cannot keep still,

its waters cast up mire and dirt.

There is no peace, saith my God, for the wicked.

Isaiah 57: 19-21

CHAPTER 1

HE WOULD BE LATE, SURELY. Nashe had warned his father to expect it, but he knew he would not be pleased. A Seder begins at sundown. There was no way around it. Nashe gazed out the window. The sun was low in the sky. Lights in the neighboring buildings were coming on one by one. Below, on the street, a swarm of pedestrians crowded the broad zebra-striped crosswalks, swirling and scattering in every direction.

Nashe turned back and gazed at the enormous room, a dim packed hall swarming with ghost-lit figures — scientists, journalists, diplomats — revolving endlessly round and round, while the afternoon sunlight, piercing the blinds, sliced them all to ribbons.

Nashe re-focussed his attention. That was one thing he could do. He was patient by nature. And take notes, endless notes, jotted down almost automatically, while his mind might be wandering practically anywhere. He transcribed what he heard:

> *...preparation for management planning of trans-boundary biodiversity conservation in the Laos Protected Forest Complex employing geo-informatics technologies and maximum entropy methods marking species distributions with presence-only data...*

Oh, God! Nashe thought, how long must I endure this Hell? The conference had been going on for three days. This was the last. Nashe would write a report as usual for his department – a troubling reflection, since what Nashe concluded never exactly coincided with what anyone had actually said. Some force beyond Nashe's control compelled him to reinterpret everything with a predictably sinister difference.

> *...The LFPC buffer zone contains 137 villages populated by ninety three thousand inhabitants. The major occupations are agriculture, fishing, and livestock grazing. Adjacent to the southern zone is*

the Cambodian Protected Forest for Conservation
of Genetic Resources of Plants and Wildlife, an area
of some 1,900 square kilometers…

Nashe knew, or at least thought he knew, where this endless, pointless talk was heading. Much of it had been determined by the very make-up of the participants themselves, which his own department had a hand in organizing. As always, there was the push from developed nations to protect the natural environment in primitive and untouched parts of the globe. But nothing was quite as simple as that. Immediate political needs as well as expectations for the future determined what could be thought, and said, and acted upon. The difficulty, from Nashe's point of view, was to determine precisely what might be of interest to his superiors and then confine his report exclusively to what they wanted to hear. After he had done that, Nashe could easily forget that the whole thing had ever happened, since, he had learned over many years of service, there was nothing he could do about it, anyway.

…this approach extrapolates known habitat
requirements to the special distributions of habitat
factors such as food, cover, water, and space derived

from cloud-free multi-temporal Landsat digital imaging, extracted and mosaiced using ERDAS Imaging software. Unfortunately, little to nothing is known about biodiversity use and management at village level in the region…

"Mosaiced." That was a new one. Nashe wrote it down. Yes, he thought, he would mosaic images of his own, constructing a picture that made sense from one perspective and one perspective only, any apparent contradictions and inconsistencies artfully shut out.

Nashe paused for a moment from his transcription. An idea struck him. He flipped back quickly through notes he had taken before the conference began. Shortly, he found it:

…all newspapers are published by the government… the sole legal political party is the communist Laos People's Revolutionary Party (LPRP)… the nation ranks: Global Peace Index (lowest quintile), Worldwide Press Freedom Index (lowest quintile), Transparency/Corruption Index (lowest quintile), Freedom and Human Development Index (lowest quintile)…

He skipped ahead and read:

…the government has set aside 23% of the nation's total land area for habitat conservation and preservation…

Twenty three percent. That's quite a chunk. Why, Nashe wondered, why this lone island of enlightenment on the part of the People's Revolutionary Party? What are they really after? Nashe did not know, perhaps would never know, but what he was sure of was this: no one wanted him, or anyone else, to explore that particular question.

Yet another speaker took the podium. Nashe had assumed the conference was approaching its close, but he was wrong. He checked his watch. The Seder would begin in fifteen minutes. No hope of making it now. His father would ask why he had to attend this conference at all, since the topic was not his specialty. The sun was almost touching the horizon, blindingly bright before it went down.

… The Laos forest is the most heavily bombed terrain in the world, having endured continuous aerial assault from 1964 to 1973 during the Vietnam conflict. Unexploded bombs in the fields and forests are estimated to number over 60 million. As eighty

percent of the population supports itself through subsistence farming, civilian casualties are common and on-going…

Yes, yes, and have been for more than half a century, Nashe thought impatiently. But what is anybody supposed to do about that now? Only a tiny portion of the warheads could ever be located and disarmed, and how many technicians would have to die in the attempt? Goodness, Nashe thought, you can get yourself killed stepping into a car, or onto a snake, depending on where you happen to live. According to the figures, which Nashe doubted anyway, a dozen or more bombs must have exploded during the three days of this very conference. Women and children killed. Their bodies ripped to bloody bits. Who knew and who cared?

Nashe stared again out the window and squinted into the departing sun till it burned his sight away. He took no pride in his cynicism. Yet sometimes Nashe toyed with the idea that he had turned actually, authentically evil. He was frequently possessed by thoughts and feelings that he dared not share with anyone. In the moments when he bothered to ponder it, Nashe guessed that this internal nastiness of his was the manifestation of some deeply buried fear or pain or hatred that he had long repressed and no longer had the strength or courage to bring to light.

As soon as the last speaker concluded, Nashe tossed his papers into his briefcase. Rather than wait for the elevator, he walked quickly down the stairs. Crossing the lobby, Nashe was surprised to find it already crowded with people formed into tight, animated circles discussing the meeting, exchanging cards, proposing future ventures. Nashe had no time and no interest in any of that. Indeed he felt as he pushed his way through the thronging mass that there was no one and nothing that tied him to anything. It was with relief that he stepped through the front door and onto the plaza. A long row of flags on either side fluttered and flapped loudly and aimlessly in the stiff breeze. He stepped beyond the line of taxicabs, put the sound of the flags behind him, and set out alone up the long, desolate hill towards the underground. The evening air was still warm as he gazed up into the dense dark sky. There was nothing to see. The clouds had shut out the stars.

CHAPTER 2

NASHE PREFERRED TO TRAVEL BY foot as much as possible, and he regularly navigated neighborhoods that his colleagues considered dangerous in the extreme. He had reached the point where he routinely lied about it: it was easier than having to explain. He had been mugged four, maybe five times. He was physically big and fought back, so he wasn't even sure if mugging was the correct term. Perhaps simply attacked. Once, a group of five or six boys who ran up behind him and banged him across the back with a stick. He chased them off. Another time, a group of three or four boys who walked directly up to him and struck him on the forehead with a bottle. It hurt but didn't break the skin. The boys ran away.

"You'll get yourself killed," people said to him, which is why he stopped talking about it. He had to admit to himself that he really did not care. So what if they killed him, knifed him, shot him? What difference would it make? Better to die violently and quickly, Nashe felt, smashed and bleeding on some filthy street, than rotting away old and helpless in a ghastly hospital, stinking of your own piss. Besides, the threat of danger stimulated Nashe, made him feel momentarily alive, as though he did not know he had a heart unless it was pounding.

It was not long before Nashe sensed trouble: only a block ahead, two men seemingly drunk, shouting and circling each other. Did he dare pass on? One of the men gazed down the street, waved his arms wildly, and screamed something in Nashe's direction. That decided it. Nashe hadn't yet reached the end of the block, so he was able to turn left at the corner and head south. Unfortunately, as he well knew, side streets are more dangerous than main avenues, and this was no exception: almost immediately he spotted a group of young men laughing and shouting a few dozen yards ahead. It was too late to change sides of the street without insult. He would have to walk it through. He appeared calm because he found quite suddenly that he was calm: he had learned over the years that there was no way of predicting how his body would react to these situations. A boy sidled up to him with a baseball bat in his hands and banged it insanely on the pavement. The bat made a loud cracking sound as if it would break in two but did not. The boy slammed it to the ground a second time. Then a third. Once again the sharp, shattering report. Nashe approached a street lamp. The boy ran up quickly and swung the bat, this time towards Nashe's head, but he rattled the intervening lamp post instead. So that was it, Nashe thought. He's afraid to hit me. He only wants to scare me. Nashe walked on. The boy, no longer pursuing him, let out a startling howl of mockery and defiance.

Nashe guessed that by taking a right at the end of the block, he would be headed once again towards his goal, but the street he now entered soon veered off at an oblique angle to the left. As far as he could tell, it was completely empty. He picked up his pace, though he worried he was now moving in the wrong direction. One block then another passed without incident, but he soon became winded. When at last he reached the crest of a small hill he paused to look back over the path he had traveled. He was high enough now to pick out in the distance the top floors of the building where he worked, and then, beyond that, the heart of the city, dimly aglow in the reflected light of the street lamps. Nashe once again turned his eyes upward but could see nothing: there were no stars or moon in the sky. He looked around himself again. He had never been in this region before. The air felt cooler and the breeze was starting to settle. The universe became, for a moment, surprisingly quiet and still.

Nashe's pulse and breathing had come back to normal. He found the spur of an alley to his left, and took it. It was rather narrow and he could not see it to the end, but he felt confident that at least he would have the path to himself. At the first bend it turned downhill slightly, and soon at a second bend led to a small set of stairs going down. There was a street light at the end which signaled some kind of intersection. He followed it and, sure enough, after one more block, made out a large open square with an entrance to the underground on the far side, though not the station he had been looking for.

Nashe hesitated a moment and glanced around. He spotted a young woman crossing the square from the right, then soon after a man from the left, both drifting sullenly towards the gate. Nashe moved into the darkness of a shadow to observe them. The man slowed his pace so that the woman could descend before him. The woman did not look up but through some invisible sign indicated that she did not wish to enter until the man stepped down first. He did so and disappeared into the portal. After a pause of several seconds, the woman straightened herself, looked completely around, and, sensing no one nearby, rushed headlong down the stairs. Now, it was Nashe's turn. He crossed the square slowly, reached the gate, sucked in one last deep lungful of the damp night air, and began his descent.

CHAPTER 3

NASHE WASN'T ABLE TO EXPLAIN to his father why he had to work on Passover. The truth was that no one in Nashe's department, even after twenty-five years, suspected that he was Jewish. He assumed that this was true as well, in a minor way, for all of his aunts and uncles and cousins.

Nashe gazed round the room at his family. Blondes predominated. Half the eyes were blue, the rest green. Most of the men were over six feet tall. The family face comprised high cheekbones, short noses, and the "Nashe chin," as his cousins called it: strong, almost jutting, and square. The family roots lay in Petersburg. Probably there had been a contribution of the very earliest Russian, which really meant Scandinavian, blood into the mix.

The family name was Nachevsky but had been changed by Nashe's grandfather Alexander, who was referred to in the family as Sasha. Sasha was educated in the Imperial Gymnasium founded by the Czar. Although unusual, it was not unheard of for Jews to be admitted. The education was classical, which meant primarily linguistic: Greek, Latin, German, and French. With special insight, Sasha's father had his sons also trained in Italian, sending them in the evenings to a school run by the Italian consulate. After the Gymnasium, Sasha entered the Technical University studying engineering. Then came the revolution. As soon as Sasha had his degree in hand, he and his younger brother Andrei booked a liner to New York.

As it happened, the one language Sasha did not know at that time was English. He bought himself a handbook and studied on the voyage over. It didn't matter. Sasha landed a job in New Haven, Connecticut overseeing a factory in which almost all of the workers were Italian. Apparently, he was the only engineer in the plant who could talk to them.

Sasha's mastery of French was a source of pride in the family, as it is for all educated Russians, and Sasha insisted that his children learn the language. After three generations, the tradition had more or less died out, but Nashe could remember as a child listening to his grandfather and uncles carrying on conversations in the language, and his cousins, down to the present day — at least the women — sometimes huddled discretely in a corner to chatter quietly and briefly in French.

No one in the family knew Yiddish, any more than they would know Turkish or Chinese. Nashe was all of thirteen when he came home and had to ask his mother what the word "goy" meant. "Where did you hear it?" his mother inquired. At school, he replied. "Well," his mother said, "it's a derogatory term that some Jews use to describe non-Jews, but it isn't a nice word, and no nice person would use it."

The family embraced life in their new country and did well. Sasha founded a manufacturing firm, building a factory and employing about two hundred workers, men and women of all races and backgrounds. When the war came, Nashe's uncles were commissioned as officers and fought against the Nazis. In Nashe's generation, all of his cousins were educated, professional people working in a variety of different fields. They enjoyed nature and the outdoors and spent summers together in a small group of cabins in the mountains.

The family never actively denied its Jewish ancestry, but clearly, Nashe felt, forces were at work that were difficult to define. Nashe remembered a temple his family joined when he was a child. Almost immediately, they stopped. When Nashe asked why, his mother smiled sweetly and said, "Oh, the men went to services in shirt sleeves and open collars." It took Nashe's mother several more years to find a suitable congregation, one where jackets and ties were required but yarmulkes were not. Once again, they stopped attending soon after, for no specified reason.

When Nashe turned fourteen his mother set about finding a boarding school for him. She was not impressed by schools that boasted how rigorous their academic programs were or that their graduates attended the best colleges. She was equally indifferent to the wealth and presumed status of the parents. What Nashe's mother wanted was a school where her son would associate with what she called "nice people." She found precisely what she was looking for, and Nashe fully enjoyed his four years at school. His teachers were patient, polite, and well-dressed gentlemen. His schoolmates were open, friendly, and kind. Nashe never felt the need to conceal his religious background, and, on the rare occasions when the subject came up, he told the truth. It didn't make any difference.

From there for Nashe it was college, then military service, and then twenty five years at the agency. He was proud of his family and their history, but as to religion it seemed to Nashe an obscure, outmoded ritual, one he hardly understood but which gave him and his family an opportunity to see each other several times a year and enjoy each other's company. That was, Nashe thought, good enough.

CHAPTER 4

MIREILLE JEMMOT WAS BORN ON the island of Barbados. Her mother was a large, tidy, conscientious woman who ran a shop selling shirts and dresses to tourists. Her father was a happy-go-lucky gentleman who drove a taxicab. Her family was of modest means, but among their neighbors and friends they were regarded as solid, industrious, outgoing people.

Mireille grew up to be a smart child and her teachers saw great things in her future. They told her parents early on to start saving for college, which they did. When she finished high school, Mireille's grades and scores were the highest possible, and she was accepted to what we call in this country an Ivy League college — indeed, to what is often considered the top Ivy League college. Her church awarded her a scholarship. Her city gave her a grant. She was a source of pride among her community and became somewhat of a local celebrity. She was excited and ready to go.

Almost immediately, however, upon arriving at college, Mireille felt she had made a serious mistake. Her new classmates seemed never to have met a young woman like her before, and in ways both direct and indirect they made known to her that her status was not, and could not be, the same as theirs. More than a few students said plainly that she could not have been admitted except for her color. Others begrudged that their own parents had to pay the way for scholarship students such as herself, although they did not. Everywhere Mireille turned, she faced incomprehension and suspicion. Her pride was hurt, and at the end of the year she deserted this prestigious institution to enroll at another highly regarded but not quite as exalted university.

Nashe was a member of the hiring committee that had brought Jemmot into the agency, and she began in his department. He mentored her during her first year, understanding from the start that she would eventually be taken out of his hands. Indeed, she rose quickly through the ranks, while Nashe, to his surprise and mortification, progressively fell. She now directed a large division of which Nashe's department, a department he no longer supervised, was a small and one could say insignificant subset.

"Oh, Nashe, Nashe, Nashe," Jemmot laughed warmly, "what are we going to do with you?"

Nashe indicated that he did not know what she meant.

"Your report has created quite the little tempest," Jemmot explained, still with a bright note in her voice. "We met just this morning. Nobody knows quite what to make of it."

Nashe was bewildered, and said so. The report seemed fairly routine to him so far as he could tell. He had submitted literally hundreds like it before.

"That's just the point!" Jemmot laughed again, even more delightedly than before. "Everything is different now! The old system doesn't work anymore. We must keep up! There is so much happening, so much progress, so many new things going on. You've been to the workshops. I know," she laughed, "because I organized them. I signed you in."

Nashe, now laughing himself, said he remembered.

"It is quite serious," Jemmot continued, changing her tone only slightly, "it's more than cosmetics. There has been a long, long history of inequity and injustice. Change is *long* since overdue. It means a very different direction for the future. It's going to be difficult," Jemmot said, looking at Nashe sympathetically, "especially for the — how should I put it — more experienced members of the agency, but there isn't any option. We all need to be onboard. It's the way it has to be."

CHAPTER 5

MAGGIE KLEIST WAS A SHORT, stout, middle-aged woman with blunt, unattractive features but a mischievous glint in her eye and a personality that other women found attractive. She had run through a long succession of partners and lovers before settling down with a tall, brilliant Australian woman, a dynamic and successful entrepreneur. They purchased a large, lovely apartment and, as soon as the laws allowed it, became legally married. A year or so after that, Maggie met the woman she believed to be the true love of her life.

Tina McCann was a petite, lively, exceptionally pretty girl who sprang from a working class Irish family in New England, a family that expelled her forever at the age of eighteen when she told them she was lesbian. Entirely on her own, Tina managed to work her way through college and then medical school. When Maggie first saw her, Tina was already in her third year of residency at a nearby hospital, but she looked, to Maggie's eyes, a mere teenager. Maggie was instantly captivated and, with her usual charm and wit, soon captivated her new friend. They became secret lovers almost at once, and a short time later Maggie confessed everything to her wife and declared she wanted a divorce.

Maggie was lucky enough to have inherited a substantial fortune from her parents. Without blinking an eye, she bought a brand new apartment, just as fine as the one she had left, where she and Tina would live. For a few blissful months Maggie thought that she was in heaven, but quite soon her relationship and her life fell to pieces.

Tina worked long and unpredictable hours at the hospital. One evening she came home later than usual. She had been drinking. When asked, she said she had been out with friends, nurses from work. Maggie slapped Tina hard across the face.

Maggie began to spy on Tina. One night, she followed Tina from the hospital as she walked with three nurses to a pub. They were all young and pretty. Maggie wandered home stunned. When Tina arrived, Maggie struck her hard with her fist, catching her on the side of the head. A fury inside of her was unleashed. She knew that she was ugly! Why had God made her this way? She knew she hardly deserved a lover as wonderful and beautiful as Tina. Tina was her one impossible dream come true, and now she was losing her, losing her to other women. It was unbearable! Maggie struck her again and again and again.

And Tina? Something inside of her finally broke. Tina, who had been strong and independent all her life, collapsed to her knees, her face on the floor, arms wrapped around her head, sobbing uncontrollably. Maggie stood above her, fists clenching and unclenching, eyes blinking. All Maggie could think, over and over, was "I am losing my mind. I am losing my mind."

Tina packed that night and left.

A few months later, an old friend invited Maggie over to see her new baby. Helping around the apartment was a live-in nurse, maid, cook, and companion named Makeena Onyango, who asked to be called Hope. She was quiet, attentive, unassuming, and pretty. After the visit, Maggie called her friend to ask if she could invite Hope to lunch.

Hope had been born in a small village in Kenya. When she refused a match with a young man and intimated that she preferred women to men, she was banned not only from her family but from the village. She moved to Nairobi, where she lived in a boarding house, found a job as a clerk in a travel agency, and became involved in the city's nascent gay community, soon becoming one its leaders. She helped organize the first ever Pride March, but the marchers were violently attacked. She met with the chief of police the next day to demand better security in the future. The chief of police said to her these exact words: "You and your kind are better off dead."

Hope began to receive death threats on the telephone, first at home, then at work. One afternoon a strange man followed her to the boarding house and punched her in the back of the neck, knocking her to the ground. Fearing for her life, Hope fled to this country.

Maggie and Hope fell in love and were soon married. Within a year Hope bore the couple a bi-racial child, a little boy, with the help of a donor Maggie had arranged. The new family settled in comfortably, and for the first time in her life Maggie experienced a feeling of real peace. Hope cared for the child and tended the apartment, while

Maggie rededicated herself to her career, enjoying her work more and more, and advancing quickly within the agency. The highlight of Maggie's day was coming home after work to rest on her bed and hold the new baby in her arms.

"How long have you been at this?" Maggie Kleist demanded of Nashe when she called him into her office. "Are you new here? You don't look it. We have a style manual, you know. Did you read it? I won't believe you if you say you did. These errors are inexcusable. And so simple-minded! It's like you are *purposely* trying to be offensive. You should be fired for incompetence, or … or maybe insubordination." Kleist smiled briefly to herself. "I guess it really doesn't matter either way.

"Your language is aggressive, exclusionary, repressive. I really can't believe it!" Kleist laughed out loud. "Why would someone give this job to *you*? You don't have the training, the background, the attitude, anything! You are unfit in every way. I mean, look at this!" She held up a page of the report. "I see multiple errors in every line! This is the kind of writing that leads to violence. Don't you realize how harmful these words can be?

"Your sense of privilege is insurmountable. It rings on every page! You are not able to see things outside your own perspective. The other for you is always, and only, the other. It's like we are all pulling in one direction, and you are sabotaging us from the other. This isn't just bad, it's *damaging*. It hurts us, it hurts the mission, but most of all it has the serious potential of hurting the people we are pledged to help all around the globe. Didn't you ever think of that? Do you even understand how much harm you are doing?

"I don't see the point in your trying to revise this. You shouldn't be working on it *at all*. That's *more* than obvious. I don't know what the others will say. *My* mind is made up: this report needs to be taken out of your hands immediately, before you do even more harm."

CHAPTER 6

JUN LI HUAN'S GRANDFATHER ZHANG Huan was a colonel in the Kuomintang air force flying missions against the Red Army. When the war ended, Zhang Huan feared the Maoists would execute him if captured and send his wife and son to a re-education camp. The ports and borders had been sealed, so, working in a garden shed, Huan built a wooden raft which he launched at night into the Ma Wan Channel. Swimming behind it, with his wife and son on board, Huan pushed the raft through six miles of open sea before landing on the shores of Hong Kong. From there Huan procured a boat to take them to safety in Taiwan.

Jun Li herself was born in Milan, Italy. Her father, who worked for an electronics firm, was the director of European sales. Jun Li became fluent in Italian, studied opera, ballet, piano, as well as the usual academic subjects. She once danced and sang as a child in the chorus of La Scala. When she was ten, her father was transferred to Paris, at thirteen to Stockholm. As an adult, Jun Li would work hard to keep up all of her languages, but she often regretted that her Swedish was somewhat shaky.

Jun Li progressed smoothly through life until the age of fifteen, when her father was transferred to California. There something happened which Jun Li was never to understand. Her father deserted them. Are you divorced? Jun Li asked her mother. No. Is he coming back? No. Do you know why? No.

Jun Li, who now called herself June, worked hard in high school, attended an Ivy League university, and graduated with honors. The first thing she did after college was fly to Taiwan to reconnect with her grandfather, then a very old man. She had the idea of writing her grandfather's biography, but in this she was profoundly disappointed. Her grandfather refused to tell her anything at all about his activities in China. He gave her no explanation.

Back in this country, June earned a PhD in International Relations and was hired by the agency immediately after. She was still relatively new.

"I've read your report," June Huan said to Nashe, "and I can see that you have given it your best effort. There is a lot here that can be salvaged and put to good use. So you should feel confident about that. Do you? I want you to understand that we will work together. I will help you. I'm sure we can put this back into submittable form. Does that sound all right to you?

"Let's start with your sources. Most of them are quite old and therefore unreliable, probably one or two generations of scholarship out of date. I'm sorry, are you not acquainted with that concept? We will have to take them out and replace them with new ones. I have attached a full list of sources for you, here."

"Now let's look at some of the specific problem areas. As a descriptor, here, you have the word bases. Our country had no bases in the Hmong areas. Bases implies a center of operations or headquarters, but we had no headquarters there. The correct descriptor is outpost. You see I have made this change for you, with the proper references here, here, and here.

"On the same page you refer to the Hmong as refugees. This was not the official determination at the time. The correct designation is domestic terrorists. You will find the documentation here, here, here, and here.

"On the following page you refer to concentration camps. The Laos government ran no camps in the county. The official term is seminars. You can find the references here and here.

"As you can see, corrections follow in the same order throughout. They fall into three categories: descriptors, data, and interpretation. There are fifty seven in the first group, fifty one in the second, and thirty five in the third, for a total of one-hundred and forty three. I have made a spread sheet for you with page references, here. Your report is rather on the short side, only fifty four pages in total, so I expect you will be able to make all the necessary corrections by tomorrow morning, when we need it for the meeting."

CHAPTER 7

IAN VAZQUEZ'S FATHER OWNED A small news shop in San Juan, and Ian's favorite time of day was coming home from school, stocking the magazine racks in the shop, choosing whatever magazines caught his fancy, and sitting on a wooden box on the sidewalk to read. Ian felt as though he had found the best of all possible worlds — indeed, two worlds wrapped up in one: the first, filled with exciting, interesting people passing before his eyes on the street, and the second, flashing astonishing, unheard of ideas into his head.

When Ian was sixteen, a young man visiting the shop noticed him reading *El Machete,* a radical publication of the time, and started a conversation. The man was impressed by Ian's mastery of Marxist philosophy. Ian could recite large swaths of the *Communist Manifesto* by heart. The man returned often. One day he asked Ian if he would hold an envelope to be picked up later by another man. He gave Ian elaborate instructions which Ian carried out to perfection. A short time later, the man invited Ian to lunch in a small restaurant on the edge of the city.

After Ian graduated from high school, the young man drove him into the jungle to a secret training ground for the Puerto Rican Liberation Army, the FALN. Ian knew very well who they were, as their activities had been prominent in the news all his life. After training, Ian was assigned to a group of four soldiers who met rarely but always wearing ski masks and using code names. Ian could be passing them on the street any day and would not recognize them.

Because Ian owned a car, an old, beat-up Datsun, and held a steady job in a fixed location, his father's shop, he was most valuable to the organization right where he was. He took the role of post office and delivery service. He kept a ski mask and a small, cheap .22 calibre revolver locked in the glove compartment of his car.

Ian followed the activity of the FALN the same way everyone else did: by reading about it in the newspapers. After six months with the organization, Ian noticed that bombings in New York, Boston, and Chicago had increased both in frequency and destructiveness. Also, the arrests of FALN soldiers. Soon, Ian found himself on a flight to New York. He was given money to find an apartment and was told to enroll in classes at the City College of New York, which was free for qualified students. Ian bought another beat-up car and every week or two was called upon to transport heavy cardboard boxes filled, he assumed, with explosives.

Then things happened very quickly. Two massive bombings with significant casualties. Large scale arrests of the FALN leadership, one shot dead by police. Payments stopped. No contact from his squad leader week after week. Ian was scared shitless. He took a job delivering Chinese food and continued to attend his college courses, which he actually enjoyed and found rather easy. He removed the ski mask from the glove compartment and threw it in the trash.

It was another three months before Ian saw his squad leader again. He asked Ian what he had been up to. Ian told him. That's good, his leader said. We need more educated people.

Over the course of the next ten years, Ian completed his undergraduate and graduate courses and earned a PhD in Political Science, writing a dissertation on the causes of revolution. He taught briefly as an adjunct professor, and then applied for a job with the agency. He moved out of New York and left his revolutionary activities behind him. He got married, divorced, married a second time, and had two small daughters whom he adored. The family lived in a modest, cozy home filled with books, and every evening after dinner Ian retired to a small study which held an impressive collection of single malt scotches and premium cigars. There, Ian would read, and smoke, and sip, and reflect on his life and feel very lucky.

Vazquez and Nashe knew each other by sight but neither could remember if they had ever actually met. They came to the conclusion that they might have been assigned to some committee together in the distant past, but were not quite sure.

"Okay, so how do I want to do this?" Vazquez began. "Politics, it's like…well….no. Let me try this another way. You have this report, right? Ten people read it, they interpret it ten different ways. They talk to each other, now you have ten to the tenth. Even if they say they agree, they really don't. Not exactly. They just agree to disagree. But what they really feel, what really triggers them, is still down there, underneath. They don't *think* the other guy is wrong, because they don't think it. They feel it. It's a purely emotional reaction. It goes right down to the deepest centers of the brain. The truth is that people have this tremendous ability to sense what is in their best, personal interest, or not, and acting on it, even when they aren't consciously aware of it and can't consciously articulate it. So that's what you're up against. You've triggered a threat response, and there's no way to correct that. You can't tell people they're not feeling what they're feeling. That's a completely losing proposition.

"And you can't analyze it, either. It's like shining a light into the messiest part of their lives. Why should they let you do that? That's a bigger threat than whatever it was that set them off in the first place. No. People don't need to be told, rationally, that there's no rational basis for their feelings. *They* don't understand how and why and just what terrifies them. You think they're going to let *you* in there?

"But that doesn't mean you can't find out. You just can't ask. In fact, you just can't do anything. It's Freud sitting back behind where they can't see, saying nothing. They have a void, so they fill it. They fill it with themselves. You let them explore the space on their own, and you pick up the pattern of what comes out.

"Nobody wants to be revealed, but it's amazing what they will reveal by themselves, if you just let them.

"You see, if you change *your* position, then that ten to the tenth gets factored again, and you'll *never* know what anything means. What you have to do is stay right in one place and let the other elements move around you, like constellations in space. Then you can triangulate everyone's position one by one against everyone else's. That's the only way you can figure out what you're up against.

"So, this is what I suggest: resubmit your report, but don't change a thing. No, I mean it. Don't change anything at all. Look, most of them probably haven't read it anyway. Maybe some did, but they weren't paying attention, or didn't understand. Others did, but when they read it again they'll say Is that what I read the first time? They won't be sure. And — here's the real point — they will be different people from who they were before. Whatever they reacted to the first time won't feel the same to them now. They'll begin to question themselves, which is exactly what you want.

"Sure, maybe one or two people will guess what you're doing, but those are the ones you don't have to worry about. They're not going to say anything because that would let everyone else know where they're coming from."

CHAPTER 8

Nashe took Vazquez's advice and resubmitted his report in its original form and then left for the day. Mid-morning next day, Nashe's department chief Charlie Emlen appeared at the door of his office.

Charlie Emlen was descended from an English family that had purchased its land from William Penn and sailed to this country in the late seventeenth century. His fifth great-grandfather was a major in the Revolutionary War. His great-grandfather was a Rough Rider who served under Teddy Roosevelt in the Spanish American War and later rose to the rank of general in the Marines. His grandfather converted a derelict metal fabricating plant into one of the largest producers of artillery shells in the Second World War. His father was a lawyer who served in the State Department under Eisenhower. Emlen was outspokenly proud of his country, and proud of his family's role in its history.

"Wow!" Emlen said to Nashe, smiling jovially, "I've got to hand it to you. You really set them off. Right out of their minds! Very impressive. I admire that." Suppressing a laugh, Emlen stepped into Nashe's office and closed the door behind him.

"Of course I can't tell you what went on in there, so I'm not, and you didn't hear it from me. But wow, what a madhouse! Jemmot had all she could handle. The Enviro team, Political, Legal, every damn body. Unbelievable!

"And by the way, just between you and me and strictly off the record, I'd watch out for Lazarescu. She's out for your blood.

"I just don't get it. The report was perfectly routine. But some of these people are crazy. They sniff trouble everywhere. Like sharks in the water. The more they tear into it, the more frenzied they get. I told them, look, you're free to hate your country if you want to, but you've got to deal with facts.

"It's all the young people, mostly. Funny, because half of them come from screwed up countries where they had terrible lives, no freedom, active persecution. Then they come here and work and succeed and make a lot of money and they talk as though this is the worst country they've ever seen.

"It's not their fault, though, really. They're just trying to fit in. They hear the way we bash our own country non-stop and they figure that's what people do here. So, you see, they're really just trying to be polite, as strange as that may sound.

"So… I don't know if you know this, I don't think it's public, but Jemmot's been promoted to Deputy Director. I can't decide if that's a good thing or a bad thing — for us, I mean. Varne's taking her place in the division, which *is* good. I can work with him.

"Also, by the way, just to be totally candid, I was *told* to look in on you and report back. I wanted to tell them right then and there What for? He wrote a normal report that says what it says. But I knew they didn't want to hear that.

"Anyway, Southeast Asia is not my specialty — nor yours either — which makes me wonder…." Emlen paused as if to find just the right words. "I was wondering why they would give this assignment to you. Didn't that seem odd to you? I'm just wondering, do you think maybe they were setting you up for something?

"I hope you don't mind my asking that. Anyway, I brought something for you. There was a guy we used to consult with in the old days. Virgil Brinton. Great guy! You would have liked him, a true scholar. He was a Southeast Asia expert during its heyday, late sixties, early seventies. He still lives nearby. You can't give him any details, but he knows a hell of a lot and could maybe give you some perspective. Of course the people who are up in arms don't give a damn about facts, but it never hurts to know more than your opponents.

"I kept the file we had on him. You can use it but don't let anyone see it. I was supposed to digitize it and destroy it with the other files, but I didn't. If you like, you can meet and pick his brains. He might be able to tell you what all this fuss is about. Let me know what he says, if you want to. I'm as much in the dark as you."

CHAPTER 9

WITH THE FILE EMLEN HAD given him, and information he found online, Nashe cobbled together a mental picture of Virgil Brinton. He, like Emlen, was the descendant of a family that settled in this country in the seventeenth century. They owned a two hundred and forty acre estate on the north bank of Crumb Creek outside Philadelphia. There was a large house, still standing, as well as an historic mill, originally for grain, later converted to paper, which became a source of considerable income. There were indications of an early connection on the maternal side with the Earl of Longford.

In more recent times, a park in the family name given to the city in the nineteenth century. A medical society, which later developed into a hospital, endowed by the family and on the board of which sat a Virgil Brinton.

Included in the file from Emlen was a journal article authored by Brinton in *Foreign Affairs,* and a transcript of testimony he had given before a congressional committee. Both pertained to the treatment of Hmong refugees after the end of the Vietnam conflict.

Nashe placed a call, introduced himself, and suggested a meeting in the lobby of a hotel in the city that afternoon. Brinton agreed, speaking in a voice that Nashe found charming, serene, and intelligent.

Nashe arrived at the hotel early and sat in the lobby until the appointed time. He observed the other guests carefully, but nobody matched the description he had formed in his mind. He checked his watch more than once, when an older gentleman whom Nashe noticed sitting at the opposite end of the room rose from his chair and walked with lively steps across the lobby in Nashe's direction. He was trim, neat, very well dressed, wearing a scholarly looking tweed jacket, knit tie, grey slacks, and steel rimmed glasses. His light reddish grey hair was cut short, and his cheeks were lightly freckled. He smiled rather sweetly and introduced himself as Virgil Brinton. He appeared exactly as Nashe had imagined him, with one exception: Virgil Brinton was an extremely light-skinned black man.

Nashe invited Brinton to sit down and explained, in general terms, that he wished to learn about the Hmong refugee issue of half a century ago, suggesting that the topic appeared to be a point of contention in the present day, although Nashe did not know why.

"Well, yes. I don't know how much you know of the history," Brinton began. "One could take it back a hundred years or more, but let's begin with the withdrawal of the French and the expansion of the Chinese into Laos and Vietnam. After the signing of the Geneva Accords in 1954, Eisenhower believed that the Vietcong would never cross the Demilitarized Zone established by that conference, and in this he was entirely correct. They never did. But they continued to supply their troops in the south by traveling through Laos and Cambodia, on what everyone referred to as the Ho Chi Minh trail. Laos and Cambodia were, of course, independent states, and, in the case of Laos, a state of declared neutrality. This fact gave Eisenhower the legitimate pretext to support Laos in the preservation of that neutrality. He began by building bases in northern Laos — yes, full fledged bases, with landing strips, supply depots, barracks. At first there were only a dozen, but by the end over three hundred. The fact that they were secret did not imply that they were in any regard illegitimate in terms of the Accords.

"What Eisenhower believed was that you don't expose your own men to danger when the enemy is starving in place where it is. The Laos bases effectively cut off Vietcong supplies to the south and stalled the offensive. It was our belief that this standstill would have lasted indefinitely.

"This is where the Hmong come into the picture. The Hmong are mountain people, culturally, ethnically, and linguistically distinct from the Vietnamese to the east and the Lao to the west. Their region just happened to lie, unhappily for them, in the center of the two main Vietcong supply routes, one leading to Vientiane in Laos, and the other to Cambodia. All of the Vietcong traffic began by crossing their lands.

"The Hmong had conflicts with the the Pathet Lao in the past as well as the Vietcong, and they distrusted them both. When our people arrived offering support, the Hmong joined without hesitation, clearing land in the jungle for airstrips and building the bases. Hmong volunteers received military training and formed an army of ten thousand within a month. The Pathet Lao, when they saw what was happening, retreated without a fight. The Vietcong, who were better armed, engaged the Hmong forces for a number of weeks, but ultimately retreated to the border. That is roughly where things stood when Kennedy took over.

Kennedy had a different approach. He wanted to rebuild South Vietnam as a democratic nation, believing they would then be strong enough to resist the communists on their own. The first thing he did was remove all of the bases in Laos, pulling out our advisors, pilots, support staff, over seven hundred men in total, and halting the shipment of supplies. When Ho Chi Minh's staff told him the news one morning at breakfast, his reply was "Is it my birthday?"

North Vietnam troops flooded the region immediately, thirty thousand in the first month, almost fifty thousand by the end. This is what the Hmong were up against, and they were completely overwhelmed. Their villages were taken one by one, men of fighting age executed, women raped. They fought on bravely as best they could for another ten years, but always at a loss. This was, by the way, the reason for their employment of child soldiers, boys no older than nine or ten, who fought side by side with their grandfathers. The middle generation had been largely wiped out.

"Johnson moved the advisors back in, and Nixon increased air sorties in the region, but they were too late to stem the tide. Once the Vietcong had established themselves in the region, they weren't about to leave.

"It was not until the end of the war that my organization became involved. We were asked to look into the condition of the Hmong refugees under the Laos People's Revolutionary Party, which seized control of the government in nineteen-seventy-five. Ten percent of the Laos population had already fled the country. Our own forces had evacuated, leaving the Hmong completely undefended. If I remember correctly, there were just two men stationed in Vientiane, strictly as observers.

"The LPRP announced over the radio that the Hmong, as imperialist collaborators, would be exterminated. The Hmong expected us to return to save them, since we had always assured them that we would, but help never came. The most our government did was convince the Thais to set up refugee camps.

"The trouble for the Hmong was that getting to Thailand involved a trek clear across the country. Around a hundred thousand made the attempt, but it's hard to move a population like that, comprised mostly of women, children, and old people. Pathet Lao soldiers lined the roads, arresting men of military age and putting them in concentration camps. Oh, yes, there were camps. Very hard to find, because they were mobile. They changed location all the time. There were no fences, none were needed, since it was dense jungle. They'd work the men clearing the land, then mining — with their bare hands, I should add. When the work was done, and before the captives had time to get their bearings and figure out how to escape, they were moved to another location. As for observers like us, we never found the camps actually in operation, only evidence of mining after they left.

"The lucky ones were sent to the concentration camps. Any man suspected of being a military leader, or any man who showed signs of being educated, went at once to what were called seminars — re-education camps, but really death camps. That is where the officers were interrogated and executed. Nobody came out alive.

"There were also breeding camps. That is what they were actually called. I suppose they existed simply for the Pathet Lao soldiers two rape women. We have no evidence that children were actually born there.

"I'm sorry this is so distressing.

"One day we heard rumors of a massacre in Hin Heup, a village north of the capital. A group of refugees evidently were awaiting permission to cross the bridge over the Nam Lik river. From what we were told, they numbered about ten thousand, mostly women and children. According to the official version, which was broadcast over the radio, the Hmong attacked the bridge with explosives and the soldiers responded. That is a highly unlikely scenario.

"We went to investigate but were stopped by soldiers on the road. So we turned around and followed trails through the jungle till we hit the river, about twenty miles downstream. We waited for a fishing boat to come by, signaled the man, and offered him money, food, anything we could think of to sail us up river. He settled for sixty French francs, a pair of gloves, and a flashlight.

"We weren't on the water more than five minutes when we spotted bodies floating downriver. At first just a few, here and there, then small batches, finally a mass of corpses spread so thick that we had to push them aside with bamboo poles. In the end, we couldn't make any progress at all, the dead were so thick. Women, children, old men, babies. They clogged the river up stream as far as one could see. We estimated they were around eight hundred. So many poor dead souls; the soldiers had shot them all."

"As to your second question, why these events should be an issue now, I can only speculate, which is something I am disinclined to do, but I suspect that whatever these organizations are hoping to accomplish today depends in some measure on how they interpret what happened in the past. The problem, of course, is that a vast amount of propaganda has found its way into the historical record. Hardly anyone knows how to deal with that.

"For example, we had been carefully monitoring the government broadcasts. They were telling the Hmong they would be enslaved in the Thai camps when they got there, their women forced into prostitution. An absurd idea. Then they convinced the Thais that it was safe to let the Hmong return, so they did. There even appeared a documentary — produced in this country, I should add, and shown to Congress — which praised the Laos communists for their humane treatment of the Hmong. None of this had any basis in fact.

"Then there is the problem of language, another sticking point for scholars who don't have a knack for linguistic analysis. This is particularly so when you are dealing with a closed society, since reports that come out are either the opposite of the truth or have no meaning at all.

"For example, the Party collectivized the farmers, as Marxists always do. They eventually gave it up, reverting to a market system, only they re-named it, calling it "socialist economic accounting."

"Then they unveiled a new constitution, declaring that the Party was the sole decision-making body in the state, but they called it "Democratic Centralism.""

"Placing "social" and "democratic" in front of everything is a form of word-magic. But do they really expect us to believe it? And yet these are the kinds of verbal tricks that people fall for again and again.

"I don't know if you know of this linguistics professor in Cambridge who used to write a lot about Southeast Asia. He said back in nineteen-seventy-five that China under Mao had a truer participatory democracy than we do. The interviewer asked him what he meant. He replied that when Mao has an idea for a new policy, he sends it to every village leader in the country so that the people can discuss it and vote on it. The interviewer said And the results of the vote are always one hundred percent in favor.

The professor said That doesn't matter. The important thing is they have a voice. So the interviewer said But didn't Mao get this consensus by assassinating fourteen million village leaders who didn't agree with him? No, the professor insisted, No such episode ever took place. Then what about Vietnam? the interviewer said. Ho Chi Minh killed eighteen thousand village leaders to get the same result. Do you deny that that happened? No, I don't deny it, the professor said. We know that happened. So, the interviewer asked, can you justify the murder of eighteen thousand of your political opponents just to get a consensus you agree with? I think I remember exactly what the professor said in response. It was: Of course I don't endorse the use of violence under any circumstances. But if these village leaders were in fact an obstacle to true democracy, then, yes, I think it can be justified.

"Well, if that's what your professors are teaching, then of course people are going to be confused. That, and propaganda, and a lack of historical knowledge, may account for the reaction you are seeing."

The conversation soon came to a close. Nashe thanked Brinton for the time he had given, stood up, and shook his hand.

"Well, thank *you*, Mr. Nashe. I have very much enjoyed talking to you."

Nashe then mentioned, just by the bye, that during his research he had stumbled upon information about the Brinton family. He gave a few examples.

"Oh yes, yes, that's all true!" Brinton smiled broadly, his eyes sparkling. Then, chuckling briefly, Brinton said, "I suppose not many people are aware that the first paper money issued by this country was printed on paper invented by a black man."

CHAPTER 10

When the Soviets annexed Hungary, Sandor Tolvay's father, who was descended from a minor branch of the nobility, lost his small estate and was forced to move to Budapest. There he was housed in a derelict factory divided into tiny rooms with no ceilings. This is where Sandor grew up.

Sandor's father tried to find work, but because he had been born into privilege he was put to the bottom of every list. He did, however, receive vouchers for food.

Sandor's toys were the brackets, bolts, wires, and other refuse to be found in and around the factory building. He discovered a defunct telephone in what had been the factory office. Fascinated, he took it apart, fiddling with the wires and contacts until he got it to work. The other families housed in the factory made calls for a week before the phone company found out and disabled the number.

This got Sandor thinking. How did the phone company know that the calls had come from here? He imagined that the pulsing sounds of the phone were a code that the machinery at the phone company was able to identify. Sandor thought, Why can't I change the code? Sandor painstakingly switched the wires in the phone one by one, dialing a logical progression of numbers each time until *viola!* he heard a ring on the other end. The process worked in both directions: the phone in the office rang at odd times.

Sandor perfected his procedure over the years to where he was able to establish a working number from virtually any location. In the blackmarket economy that had sprung up in the city, Sandor found plenty of people who would pay him to set up a pirate telephone service.

When Sandor reached his final year of high school, his test scores, especially in mathematics, were the highest his teachers had ever seen. He applied to the Technical University of Budapest, but was denied. As the son of a former nobleman, his application was dropped a specified number of places down the list. He was told to try next year, which he did. And the year after that. On his fourth attempt, four months after his father passed away, Sandor was accepted.

Sandor's years at the university were the most intense of his life. He studied physics, computers, and electrical engineering, graduating at the top of his class. He applied for several jobs, but once again was denied. Sandor realized that the social demerits attached to him by the state would follow him for the rest of his life — that is, unless he left the country.

Because he had been educated at state expense, Sandor had been issued an internal passport, prohibiting him from traveling outside the city. When he applied for an external passport, he was denied. Why do you want it? the official demanded. Hungary is a beautiful country, Sandor responded. I want to see more of it.

Although not a Party member, Sandor attended auxiliary meetings every Wednesday, wearing a red kerchief round his neck, singing the *Internationale*, and listening to lectures on Marxism-Leninism. Attendance was taken. He never missed a meeting.

Three years later, after repeated attempts, Sandor Tolvay was finally granted an external passport. He had had plenty of time to prepare, so he moved quickly. The Hungarian-Austrian border was only lightly defended. The barrier itself, unlike the East German, was not armed with explosive shells. The difficulty was traversing the last few miles to the border without being detected. The rumor was there were scouts whom one could hire. The other rumor, of course, was that the security police posed as scouts to capture defectors. Sandor chose to work alone. He committed a topographical map to memory, walked only through the densest forests, and, when he believed he was near the border, started running. He was stopped by a simple chain link fence, without even barbed wire on top. He climbed over, hiked to the nearest village, and declared himself a refugee.

Sandor spent the next two months in a camp in Austria and then was given a visa and plane ticket to emigrate to this country. He settled in New Brunswick, New Jersey, found a small apartment, and worked as a technician in a machine shop. After only one year, he applied for a job with the agency. On the mathematics portion of the entrance exam, according to agency legend, Sandor Tolvay achieved the only perfect score ever recorded.

Tolvay's work on coding and counter-intelligence was brilliant, and he was offered promotion to administrative posts on several occasions. He declined each time, responding tersely "I do not trust people, only machines."

Tolvay asked Nashe to come to his office and show him his computer. Nashe sat across his desk waiting while Tolvay typed at the keyboard and peered deeply into the screen.

"Someone is in here," Tolvay said at last, then after a pause added, "I mean, in here right now."

Tolvay returned to the keyboard and typed some more, then sat back in his chair, sighed deeply, and stared at the ceiling for several minutes. "Is bad," he muttered.

"Code goes in," he reflected, "code goes out. But it is not ours! This machine has network I do not know, yet."

Tolvay looked across the desk at Nashe and added, reassuringly, "It is not you. Is too deep."

Tolvay tilted his head sideways for a few moments and decided, "I am loading program." He stretched an arm towards Nashe as if to pat him on the shoulder and said "Do not worry! I made program."

The program took several minutes to load. The two men sat in silence. Nashe asked Tolvay about the picture on the wall behind his desk. It appeared to be a grand palace on the bank of a broad river.

"Oh, this," Tolvay said, "this is my shame," and he pressed his hand to his heart. "This is my university. They told us we should do great things for our country. I left." He smiled sadly, pressing his hand to his heart again.

When the program was loaded, Tolvay handed the computer to Nashe.

"You do nothing," Tolvay advised. "I will help you. I will know who is doing this. I will find them out."

CHAPTER 11

PATRICK MORETTI'S FATHER ABANDONED HIM before he was born. He was raised by his Irish mother and grandmother and grew up to be an intelligent, devout, soft spoken, and very tall young man, six feet six, with a delicate, almost emaciated body. He entered a seminary at seventeen, intending to become a priest.

It didn't take Patrick long to figure out that one of the priests was sleeping with a number of the seminarians. He did not want to be a rat, but he had taken his vows seriously and was troubled by what he was hearing.

The more Patrick investigated the matter, the more widespread he found it to be. He couldn't decide what to do, until one day he heard a story about an older priest who was abusing young children. Patrick was profoundly upset and made an appointment to speak to the Bishop.

The Bishop welcomed Patrick into his study, and Patrick explained as fully and directly as he could what he knew. The Bishop listened intently, neither denying anything nor admitting anything. He did not threaten Patrick into silence nor encourage him to speak out. The Bishop initiated nothing, and he concluded nothing. Patrick found the conversation painful and frustrating. It was all empty talk. The next day, Patrick quit the seminary.

A year later, Patrick enrolled in the state university. This was the era of the student uprisings, and Patrick soon became deeply involved. He marched for civil rights, organized resistance to the draft, and protested against the war in Vietnam. Ultimately, the students took over the university, holding it for a period of six weeks. Patrick was one of the leaders. He spoke often at meetings and came to be relied upon for his cool head, command of facts, and practical common sense. He became a member of SDS, Students for a Democratic Society, and was secretly asked to join the Weathermen. He declined, explaining to Nashe later, "I realized that violence was not the answer."

Long after college, Patrick found himself still in demand as an activist and organizer. He lived in a one room apartment and drove a taxicab to make ends meet. He became progressively involved in movements for gay rights and gender equality, and against child exploitation and human trafficking. Patrick lived and worked in this way for the next fourteen years, but increasingly he came to feel out of touch. The younger generation spoke a different language, saw things in a different light. Patrick returned to graduate school and enrolled in a women's studies program. When asked, as he often was, why a man would be taking women's studies, Patrick would say, "Men have been telling women what to think for long enough."

Nashe and Patrick Moretti met at a party during graduate school. Exceptionally tall and thin, with long silver hair tied back in a ponytail that hung down to his waist, Moretti was impossible to miss. They struck up a conversation and became friends. Over the years, Nashe came to realize that Moretti was extremely well versed in, among other things, issues pertaining to Southeast Asia. Nashe decided to pay him a visit. Moretti suggested a meeting at a shelter where he worked.

"The country you're dealing with," Moretti began, "is the number three, maybe number two biggest source of human trafficking. I think for women, it might be number one. They're mostly sent to Thailand, Japan, China. Mostly sex work, or domestic work, sometimes factories. They're enslaved, mostly, or contract slaves.

"The most vulnerable are the ones from the poorest areas, the areas farthest north and closest to the border. Those happen to be the very same areas where they've set up these nature preserves. So that's interesting.

"I don't know what it means. I guess if they take land away from the peasants, they drive them into poverty, which feeds the trafficking. I don't know if that's profitable. Maybe they just do it for political reasons. They've been trying hard to raise capital — looking for outside investors — they probably think having nature preserves make them more attractive.

"I believe these are also the big opium growing areas. Let me check something…" Moretti turned to his computer and searched for different sorts of maps. It took him less than a minute to find what he was looking for. "Okay. So this is interesting. Here's a map of a helicopter flyover marking the opium fields. Here's another map of the protected forests. They match, see? That's interesting.

"Let's see what else we've got here… Okay. It says that international investment, especially from our country, is contingent upon their reducing the production of opium. So…. Maybe they're just hiding the opium fields in the protected areas. Just an idea.

"You know, governments like that claim to be for the people, but they exploit them just like everybody else, and we go along with it, when it's to our advantage.

"Let's see what else…There's a lot here about child sex tourism. Our own citizens seem to be number three on the list of most frequent visitors. I don't know what that means in terms of your problem. I don't think they're protecting sex tourists.

"The slavery angle is interesting, but I don't know how that fits what you've got. It's a huge issue, of course, and I'm not an expert, but we have probably ten thousand slaves in this city alone, which is pretty amazing if you think about it.

"I'm working with a woman right now, she wasn't trafficked, but she was a slave. No, really. I was talking to her when you rang the buzzer. You may have seen her going up the stairs when I got you at the door.

"Her father was a journalist in Sudan who wrote something about the government so they threw him in jail. His wife and daughter tried to visit him, and the military guy who was in charge saw her — that's the daughter — and took a fancy to her. He tortured the father to death, then went to see the girl at her home and told her he planned to make her one of his wives. Can imagine having to marry the guy who tortured and killed your father?

"She and the mother were frantic. They didn't know what to do. They were powerless to say no, but, my God! So the mother wrote some distant cousins here in the city and said she wanted to get her daughter out of the country. Could they help?

"They said Sure, send her over, we'll take care of her and make sure she finishes her education. Well, she arrived. They had her sleep in the storage room on the floor. She took care of the children, cleaned the apartment, did the laundry. Funny thing I haven't figured out is she did their laundry in the washing machine but she had to clean her own clothes in a tub. She wasn't allowed to use the machines for herself. Strange.

"She didn't eat with them. She ate the leftovers.

"After a few months of this she asked when she was going to school. That's when they started physically abusing her. She had cigarette burns under her arms and on her thighs. They never let her out of the apartment. It took her awhile to figure it out, but eventually she realized she was a slave. It took her another two months to work up the courage to escape. Six weeks ago she showed up here. She left the children in the apartment and simply ran out the door.

"She was pretty anemic when she got here, so we had that to deal with. Now a new problem has come up: some young man who's a friend of her cousin's says he saw her at the apartment and he's in love with her and will marry her if she comes back. She asked me what I thought. I asked her How well do you know this guy? Can you trust him? She said, He's a good Muslim boy. I don't think he would lie. I said, It may be he's just working for your cousin to try to lure you back.

"Well, technically I wasn't supposed to get involved like that, but she's terribly naive so I felt I had to. Now, today, she gets a letter from her mother saying that the boy is in contact with people back in Sudan, and they're threatening her. So now the girl's worried they're going to do something to her mom.

"Well, I know this isn't your problem, exactly, but it does show you one thing: once you get involved in these things, the circles always widen in all kinds of ways you never would have imagined, and everything looks like it's going to spin way out of control before it gets better."

CHAPTER 12

VIKTOR LAZARESCU AND HIS WIFE Elena had a pact never to discuss politics. He never broke it; she sometimes did. "I don't know how you can support an evil dictator like that," she would say. Women in their country were arrested for seeking abortion, or even trying to find contraceptives. Public demonstrations of all kinds were outlawed. The Securitate had more informers than any known police state in the world. No less than eleven people personally known to Viktor and Elena had been summoned to Bucharest under suspicion of anti-government activity. Three of them never returned.

In truth, Viktor was a scientist, a professor of Chemistry and Environmental Engineering, and he simply had no mind for politics. Terms without precise meaning confused and annoyed him: freedom and oppression, chaos and order, justice and injustice. When he listened to his wife, what she said sounded reasonable. When he listened to Party officials, it was the same.

Viktor knew the Party lied. He had written two research articles every year for twelve years, submitting them to the Ministry of the Environment. He never saw the articles again until they appeared in print in various scientific journals. His data had been changed, his conclusions reversed. He never complained. He never told anyone, least of all his wife.

On December the seventeenth, nineteen eighty-seven, a special courier appeared at the door of Viktor's office at the Polytechnic University of Timisoara and ordered him to sign for the receipt of a letter. It was from the Ministry of the Environment, directing him to appear before them in Bucharest on December twentieth at 10:00am. Viktor put his elbows on his desk, his head in his hands, and had to breathe deeply for several minutes to keep from passing out.

At home, Viktor asked his wife to take a walk with him in the park. Their daughter Mariana, eleven years old, was playing in the garden.

Viktor was fairly certain that his home was not bugged. The Securitate was anything but subtle. When they wanted to bug a house, they ordered the residents out and brought workmen in. The homeowners, when they returned, found wires from a telephone pole running to a newly installed box on the side of the house. Nothing of the sort had happened at the Lazarescu's, but it was always better to be careful.

Viktor quietly explained the situation. Elena grasped it at once. "Whatever you have done, do not tell me. We will not tell Mariana even that you are going to Bucharest." It was common knowledge that wives and children would be interrogated. "Whatever you were planning, if it was against this monster, I will understand."

The Securitate operated out of the Ministry of Interior, but it was common practice to call suspects in to other departments and arrest them there. They very rarely arrested anyone in their homes. Failure to comply with a summons was an admission of guilt; everyone showed up when called.

It was a twelve hour train ride from Timisoara to Bucharest, which Viktor had to pay for himself. Once at the ministry, he was taken to an office and told to sit and wait. Forty-five minutes later, three men entered the room. One he recognized as an official from the ministry, the second was introduced as a ministry worker, the third, who was not introduced at all, was the Securitate officer.

Viktor was told that in three weeks the four of them would fly to The Hague to attend a conference on atmospheric pollution in Europe. Viktor would read a paper, which they handed him. "Know it thoroughly," he was warned. "Questions will be asked. You must be prepared."

Viktor studied the paper on the train ride home. He saw immediately that the data had been fabricated. Research based on satellite data from western states suggested that there were dangerous concentrations of atmospheric carbon hovering over three industrial centers in Romania. Viktor's paper was a refutation of those claims.

"Hmm," Elena responded, when they were once again in the park, "this might be all right, but you cannot trust them. Do what they tell you to do, but keep your eyes open, and try to escape if you can. Yes, do it! Do not worry about us. We will get by."

Viktor's performance at the conference was a tremendous success. The paper itself was all right, but

Viktor's responses to questions from the panel were impressive and, more importantly, convincing. He and his team returned to their hotel to celebrate. They ordered a large meal and ate and drank late into the evening. They were all thoroughly drunk when Viktor stood up, excused himself, and stumbled to the bathroom. He never made it. At the end of a corridor he saw a door marked exit. Viktor stepped through the door onto the street, found a taxicab at the corner, and asked to be driven to the US Embassy, where he requested, and was granted, asylum.

Settled in this country, Viktor rented a single room in a rough section of a large city. He found a job as a janitor mopping floors and cleaning windows in a housing project. About a year later, when a position as building superintendent became vacant, Viktor applied and got the job. Like most men from eastern-block countries, Viktor could repair almost anything — plumbing, electrical wiring, motors, pumps, internal combustion engines. It was easy, and the position came with a basement apartment free of charge.

Viktor wrote Elena almost every day for a week, then twice a week for a month, then once every two weeks from then on. He never got a response. He assumed his letters were intercepted by the Securitate. If not, then hers were. He had defected on an impulse and because Elena told him it would be all right. Now, almost two years later, Viktor had come to believe despairingly that he would never see his wife and daughter again.

Then, a miracle happened. On December seventeenth, exactly two years after he had received his summons from the Department of the Environment, mass protests exploded in Timisoara over the arrest of a priest who had criticized the government. For the next seven days, the whole world watched as revolution spread across Romania. There were hundreds of thousands of people in the streets. The army was called in to restore order, several hundred civilians were shot dead, and then the soldiers themselves rebelled and joined the protesters. The dictator Ceausescu was arrested, accused of genocide, and, on the afternoon of Christmas Day, executed by firing squad.

A week later, Viktor received a letter from Elena. They were safe, she was in Bucharest arranging for passports. There was confusion in the government, she did not think the situation would last, but, at least for the moment, things were opening up. She would work as fast as possible to get them out. Money would help, if he could send it.

He sent every penny he had. Fourteen days later, a second letter from Elena arrived with instructions. Viktor could not believe what he was reading: Elena and Mariana would be landing in this country in two days.

Viktor cleaned his basement apartment as best he could, bought food for a meal, and then, for the first time in his life, walked into a wine store. Viktor had been thinking of a time long ago when he was a little boy and his father drove them into the country to visit his grandfather, who lived on a small farm at the foot of the mountains. The family gathered to eat around a table under a large spreading tree, and Viktor's grandfather carefully opened a bottle of a special wine called Tokaji, golden in color, which the adults drank out of delicate stemmed glasses. Viktor had never in his life tasted that wine; when the Soviets took over the country, they appropriated the vineyards, neglected to cultivate them, and shipped whatever wine was left to Russia. Viktor found a bottle of Tokaji on the shelves. Even by his own frugal standards it was inexpensive. Probably, it wasn't even a good wine. But, cradling that bottle in his hands and gazing into its bright golden depths, Viktor felt that a part of his past had been restored, and that life for himself and for his family would come around full circle at last.

The day came. Elena and Mariana arrived, happy, but exhausted, Mariana practically asleep. Viktor and Elena spoke in hushed tones and ate a little of the dinner he had prepared. Mariana, seated next to her mother, fell asleep on her shoulder. Taking great care, Viktor opened the bottle of Tokaji, poured two glasses, and held one out to his wife, which she took. Viktor wanted to say something, but he was too overcome to speak. The husband and wife looked at each other, raised their glasses, and, tears streaming down their faces, they drank.

*

Mariana Lazarescu awoke with a start. Above her, where there should have been a ceiling, were exposed rusting pipes, dangling electrical wires, and greying galvanized air ducts; below, on the floor, tool boxes, buckets of various sizes, scattered pipes and fittings, and what appeared to be parts from machinery which she could not identify. She was still in her clothes, lying on her side on a vinyl couch that was clammy to the touch and smelled like some kind of machine oil.

She sat up alarmed. Where was she? She shook her head a little, and slowly the events of the last few days came back to her. She had flown to this country, the first time she had ever been in an airplane. It was dark when they arrived. Where was her mother? There were no windows, but a dim light seeped through the bottom of a door on the opposite side of the room. Her feet were bare and the floor was cold and dirty-feeling. She lifted her feet off the concrete, hugged her knees to her chest, and stayed like that for two hours until her parents woke up.

The family shared a simple breakfast at a small, dingy table. Her parents spoke quietly. She observed her father closely, but hardly recognized him. He was older, heavier, and looked tired. He was unshaven and wore blue soiled workman's overalls. He could have been someone else.

Mariana feigned sleepiness. Her mother took her by the hand and led her into a second room where there was a single bed and told her to lie down and rest. She and her father would wake her when they were ready to go out. Her mother closed the door halfway. Mariana heard the sound of sorting and cleaning as her parents, under the direction of her mother, started to put the apartment in order. They must have worked for several hours. Somewhere in there, Mariana drifted off to sleep.

When she woke the second time, she was hungry. She stepped out into the first room, where her parents were still working. Her father gazed at her but she tried to avoid his eye. He asked if she felt better and she shrugged. He walked over and gently put his arms around her. She reluctantly let him hold her. He smelled of dust and grease.

Mariana sat on the broken sofa and waited. When her parents were ready, she got up and walked with them to the street. It was not what she expected. Opposite to their building stood a row of small dilapidated houses of different sizes, a few of them burnt out and empty. Garbage littered the sidewalk. There was no grass to be seen, no trees, no flowers, only drab concrete and, here and there, an empty dirt lot enclosed by a chain link fence.

Back in the apartment, Mariana sat at the table stunned while her parents put away the groceries. She missed her city already. Why had they come here? Timisoara was so beautiful, with its parks and palaces, majestic cathedrals, and handsome ornate buildings on broad avenues. She lived in a pretty cottage with a large walled garden filled with fruit trees, berry bushes, and flowerbeds. They grew apples, peaches, pears, raspberries, hazelnuts. What they didn't eat they preserved in jars and enjoyed all winter. Why had her father deserted them to come to a place like this, of all places in the world, and why had they followed him?

Everything had been going so beautifully! Mariana loved her old school and her friends. Every weekend she and the Pioneers donned their uniforms and hiked in the surrounding hills, or had picnics, or picked fruit in the orchards for the farmers, or sang patriotic songs in the park for old people. They won medals for leadership, for volunteering, for sports, for achievement in school. They were encouraged to compete, and Mariana had won the most medals of all!

And then one day, Mariana's mother told her that her father had left and was not coming back. The day after that, Mariana was interrogated, alone, by the Securitate. They said her father was a criminal and a traitor to the revolution. She was asked countless questions she could not answer: Did your parents argue? What did they argue about? Who came to the house? What radio broadcasts did they listen to? She was interrogated three days in a row. When at last she returned to school, she was forced to sit alone in a back corner of the classroom because, it was announced, she was the girl whose father was an enemy of the people. But that was not the worst. The worst was that she was expelled from the Pioneers. She lost her friends, and every weekend she spent alone in her room at home.

And now, this! Living in a dungeon in the ugliest place on Earth! Why had this happened to her?

Two weeks after her arrival, Mariana was enrolled in school. She did not know the language, but she understood behavior, and what she saw shocked her literally beyond belief. A boy in the hallway walked backwards in front of her fondling his crotch and leering at her suggestively. She thought he must be simple-minded or insane. Why was he in school? Two girls pretended to ask her a question just so they could laugh at her speech. A boy in her classroom stood up and shouted at the teacher, she knew not what, until a second boy stood up shouting and chased the first boy around the room. They knocked over chairs and shoved the teacher aside, who went on talking and did nothing.

In Romania, teachers punished you if you talked out of turn, or failed to do an assignment, or even if you did an assignment but did it poorly. A hard smack on the palm with a meter stick did the job. Students were sometimes punished individually, but at the teacher's discretion the entire class might be punished for the transgression of a single student. That was most effective of all.

When Mariana arrived home from her first day and her parents asked how it had gone, she did not know how to answer at all. She had never in her life imagined anything like it.

*

Before they left Romania, Mariana's mother quickly but carefully sorted through thousands of sheets of paper. She collected Viktor's diplomas, transcripts, published articles, university ID cards, pay receipts, department memos — anything that could certify that her husband really did have a PhD and really was a professor at a prestigious university. Viktor, armed with this thick file of documents, applied for many kinds of jobs, and, after three long years of searching, finally landed one with the city department of environmental conservation working in a lab testing air samples. It looked easy, and it would pay well.

The family celebrated that night with a special dinner.

"So, you make more money now?" Mariana, now sixteen, asked.

"Yes," her father said.

"And we can move out of this place?" Mariana had often complained that she was ashamed to bring friends to the apartment.

Her parents glanced at each other nervously.

"No," her father said, "this job takes so little time, and we get the apartment free. I can do both jobs. College is very expensive in this country. It will take all the money we can get."

"Oh!" Mariana actually screamed. "Why did we come here? I hate this country! College is free in Romania!"

"But we had no freedom," her mother said.

"I don't care!"

"You are too young to understand. One day…"

"No! I don't care! I don't care about freedom! I'd rather be without freedom than live in a fucked-up place like this!"

Her mother leaned forward as if to slap her, something she had never done before.

Mariana recoiled and screamed "You can't hit me! I'll call the police! That's how it is in this shit fuck country!"

Mariana's parents were shocked, but did nothing.

Since her parents would not punish her, Mariana chose to punish her parents. By slow, deliberate stages, Mariana transformed herself into someone else, cutting fabric from her blouses, slicing holes in the legs of her pants, painting more and more garish make-up on her face, and generally trying, as she put it, "to look like a slut." She cursed and spoke freely at dinner about drugs and sex as if she were involved, although she was not, and pretended that this was normal behavior for kids in this country. Her father looked pained, her mother angry, but they endured it, and said nothing.

In school, by contrast, Mariana worked harder than ever. Her classmates teased her, but she found ways of fighting back. One time, finishing a test early, Mariana rested her elbow on her desk, put her chin in her palm, and stared fixedly at one of her tormentors, a boy who was sitting next to her, struggling with the exam. Annoyed, he demanded, "What are you looking at?" Mariana replied, "I'm watching you try to think. It's interesting."

The family now owned a car. One weekend in the spring they took a drive upstate to a large, prestigious university. It was a revelation to Mariana. The broad lawns, massive trees, and tall dignified buildings reminded her of her home city, Timisoara. She almost cried. She was introduced to students who were nice, intelligent, and, she couldn't help noticing, well dressed. She reflected on her own outfit and was ashamed. Was it possible she could go to such a university? Once back home, Mariana removed the heavy make-up and began to dress in a more sensible manner. She worked harder at school than ever before, and, ten months later, to her delight and disbelief, she was accepted to the university.

And she was ashamed of her bad behavior to her parents.

Mariana's years at the university were a whirlwind. She loved her classes, her professors, and she made good friends. No one had to know where she lived, and they found her Romanian accent exotic and chic. The boys started to pay attention. Once, sitting in the lounge, Mariana overheard a group of boys talking about her. "She's kinda hot," one boy said, "but a real ball-buster." She was definitely okay with that.

After university, Mariana attended law school. Immediately after law school, she joined the agency in the legal department. She was still relatively new.

Ms Lazarescu summoned Nashe to her office. When he arrived, she was seated behind a desk with a microphone on a stand. She instructed Nashe to sit opposite her. Behind her to the left stood a man she did not introduce.

Ms Lazarescu tapped a key on the computer and spoke into the microphone, giving a case number, the date, her name, and the name of the subject, Nashe. She then advised Nashe that the interview would be recorded and asked him to acknowledge that he had been advised as such. She paused a moment and then made an impatient forward-rolling movement with her hand as if to indicate "Well, go on, say something!" Nashe said he had been advised.

Ms Lazarescu then asked Nashe if he was aware that two television news broadcasts based on "confidential government sources" claimed that our country had a role in human rights abuses in Laos. Nashe said no, he was not aware of that.

"Mr Nashe I am handing you a transcript of the first broadcast under discussion. Would you read aloud the highlighted portions." Nashe read the portions.

"Now, Mr Nashe, will you give in your own words a summary of the import of the passage you read." Nashe did, saying that a confidential source within the government leaked classified information which indicated that our government was concealing human rights abuses in the mining industry in Laos.

"Mr Nashe, are you the confidential government source referred to in this report?" Nashe said he was not.

"Mr Nashe, do you know the identity of the confidential government source referred to in this report?" Nashe said he did not.

Ms Lazarescu handed Nashe a second transcript and asked him to read it and then summarize it. Nashe did. He said that a confidential government source claimed that government agents may be involved in human trafficking into the mining industry of Laos and the sex industry of Thailand.

Ms Lazarescu asked again, "Mr Nashe, are you the confidential government source referred to in this report?" Nashe said he was not.

"Mr Nashe, do you know the identity of the confidential government source referred to in this report?" Once again, Nashe said he did not.

Ms Lazarescu then said, "Mr Nashe, you are hereby put on notice that you are the subject of an investigation into unauthorized leaks of government information. It is my responsibility to inform you that this investigation will take place on three distinct levels.

"First: Administrative. Has subject violated policies and directives regarding protection of Sensitive But Unconfidential Information (SBU), as per Executive Order (E.O.) 13526, Intelligence Community Directive (ICD) 701, and DoD Directive (DoDD) 5210.50.

"Second: Administrative. Has subject violated policies and directives regarding protection of Classified Information, as per Executive Order (E.O.) 13526, Intelligence Community Directive (ICD) 701, and DoD Directive (DoDD) 5210.50.

"Third: Criminal. Has subject violated Title 18 of the U.S. Code, section 798, prohibiting the knowing and willful transmittal of Classified Information to an unauthorized person.

"Be advised that should findings be positive for levels one and two, you will be entitled to legal representation within the department.

"Be advised that should findings be positive for level three, you will *not* be entitled to legal representation within the department. You will be required to provide your own legal representation.

"Be advised that the penalty for violation of Title 18 of the U.S. Code, section 798 is fine or imprisonment of not more than ten years or both.

"Mr Nashe, do you understand what has been presented to you in this meeting?"

Nashe said he did.

"Mr Nashe, do you have any questions?"

Nashe said that he did not.

Ms Lazarescu collected her papers into a folder and tapped a key on the computer to stop the recording. She then looked at Nashe and said "My advice, Mr Nashe, is that you find legal representation."

CHAPTER 13

Boone Clarke from Boone County, Kentucky began his career stationed in a tree fort in Vietnam monitoring secret radio transmissions seven years after the fall of Saigon. The experience left him with a lifelong fear of spiders, since he frequently woke in the morning with a rather large spider squatting over his face.

A number of years later, Boone Clarke was the leader of an anti-piracy team operating in the Indian Ocean, protecting oil tankers sailing from the Persian Gulf. His method, clear, simple, and effective, never changed and became a model for operations around the world. First, take for granted that the ship's captain and crew have been murdered and thrown overboard. Second, attack in darkness using night-vision goggles and satellite guidance. Third: parachute from a silent-running airplane, land on the deck of the tanker, subdue all targets, and throw them overboard, dead or alive. When asked whether this last detail was necessary, Boone would laugh impishly and respond, "Nobody is missing these guys."

Some years after that, Boone was sailing a thirty-six foot yacht in the open seas to top-secret installations around the world. When he reached his destination, he would drop anchor and row a dinghy ashore, usually accompanied by an attractive female in a bikini. They would then roll out a blanket on the beach and picnic, or swim, or sunbathe, until a squad of soldiers descended upon them with M-16 rifles drawn ordering them to turn face down on the sand. At that point, Boone would stand up, smile, chuckle to himself, flash a card from his wallet, and say something like "It took you men seventeen minutes and forty three seconds to get here. We need to talk."

Presently, Boone Clarke worked stateside in that twilight world of quasi-private, quasi-public security contractors. He showed up at Nashe's office the day after his meeting with Mariana Lazarescu, walked in, smiled, sat down, chuckled briefly, and starting speaking. He didn't close the door, or mention his name, or show his identification.

"You're in a bit of trouble, they tell me," Boone said. "This new crowd doesn't like something you've written. Good luck with that." Boone laughed heartily.

"And you've been talking to civilians. Patrick Moretti. Lucky guy. Should be serving time for domestic terrorism, only they couldn't get anyone to testify against him, even after they found the pieces." Boone giggled to himself.

"Moretti was part of that Weather Underground team that blew themselves up in New York trying to make a bomb. He showed up ten minutes late. The whole townhouse was was a crater."

Nashe leaned forward at his desk but said nothing.

"Virgil Brinton, another beauty. Belonged to a private organization that was supposed to be doing relief work. He was convicted twenty years ago of human trafficking, but the sentence was commuted. They caught him by chipping the boys and girls in the camps. First time they used that technology in the field. He claimed he was sending them to schools but they ended up in brothels in Thailand."

Excuse me, Nashe interrupted, But who are you?

Boone Clarke smiled indulgently with a look that said Now, now, you know better than that.

"You met Sandor Tolvay," Boone continued and laughed warmly. "Brilliant guy. Watch out your computer doesn't melt on you, or catch fire. I'm serious about that." Boone laughed some more.

"This'll go smoothly if you don't muck it up, so do me a favor and don't talk to any more civilians. And turn your computer off except when you need it for work. Don't carry your phone, either. Need to talk to someone? Do it face to face. D'ya know how to read a map? Use a map. It's not as hard as you think, and it may keep you out of trouble."

Boone Clarke stood up, smiled broadly, chuckled softly to himself, turned on his heels, and walked briskly out the door. After he was gone, Nashe sat silently and stared into space for several minutes, sorting out what he was thinking and feeling. It was rather a lot to balance all at once. Nashe found himself sighing deeply several times. It felt good and helped him settle the agitation in his heart. Thoughts and memories began to spin through his consciousness like dead leaves driven by a swirling wind.

Nashe recalled how during graduate school he and Moretti would telephone each other when they had a break in their studies to arrange a walk around the city. No particular destination, or so Nashe thought, only the need to step out into the air and get some exercise. More often than not, these random peregrinations turned out to be not so random after all, at least from Moretti's point of view. Wandering through maze-like streets of neighborhoods Nashe had never seen before, they would frequently cross the path of a Pride March, or a student protest, or a demonstration against war or oppression or corruption or racism or sexism. Always something. And when Nashe figured out where they were and asked Moretti if he had planned all this, Moretti always denied it.

One late afternoon, Moretti told Nashe he wanted to take him someplace special. They walked for a long time until it was growing dark. Moretti told Nashe the story about how he had been asked to join the Weathermen several times but always refused. Moretti was such a naturally serene and peaceful man that Nashe never doubted him. But on this particular occasion Moretti seemed more serious and thoughtful than usual. At dusk, just before the street lamps were lit, Moretti stopped in the middle of a block, gazed over Nashe's head at the buildings behind him, and said softly "This is it."

Nashe turned around. There was nothing particularly special to see. An ordinary residential street of pleasant older homes with one rather ugly modern construction in the middle. Nashe didn't know what to say. What is it? Moretti replied simply, but with difficulty, "I knew the people who lived there. You probably heard about it in the news. They were making a bomb in the basement and it blew up. The house was completely destroyed. No one survived."

Nashe and Moretti were now standing side by side. Nashe looked the house up and down, but said nothing. Then Nashe glanced out of the corner of his eye at his friend. It was growing quite dark, and Nashe could not swear to it, but he thought he detected, for the first and only time, that there were tears in Moretti's eyes.

But how did the agency know that Nashe had spoken to Moretti? He never discussed it with anyone. And nothing Moretti said showed up in his report. Moretti himself was unlikely to talk to a government agent. But then again, Nashe thought, Who knew? Maybe he would.

Nashe had called Moretti on his phone to set up the meeting and had walked to Moretti's workplace. Obviously, that was what that man — whoever he was — was referring to about not using his phone. Given the nature of Nashe's profession, he understood how such things worked, but Nashe never imagined that this battery of surveillance would one day be turned against him.

Nashe thought about his meeting with Virgil Brinton. Although he found Brinton to be a congenial old gentleman and enjoyed talking with him, Nashe had revealed nothing compromising, and nothing Brinton said was included in his report. No, that wasn't the problem. What bothered Nashe was that the meeting had been suggested by his department chief, Charlie Emlen. This now appeared an all too obvious set-up, an attempt to entrap Nashe by seeing what he might reveal to a civilian. But what was the point of it all? Nashe had done nothing wrong. Nothing even out of the ordinary. And even if he had, why hadn't his superiors merely asked him a few simple questions? Why this clandestine, hostile, and paranoiac reaction?

Nashe recalled a story he had heard only a few days before about a young woman from China who was studying in one of our universities. The woman had remarked that she found it a breath of fresh air that in this country she could say and think whatever she liked. One of her Chinese classmates reported her comment to the Chinese Consulate, and the Consulate relayed that message to the Ministry of State Security in Beijing. The Ministry dispatched a pair of officers to visit the young woman's parents, threatening that if they could not control their daughter they would be fired from their jobs and kicked out of their apartment. Frantic, the parents phoned their daughter immediately to ask what she had done. That much of the story was bad enough. But what upset Nashe most of all was this: that the total elapsed time between when the young woman made her comment and when her parents called her in a panic from halfway around the world was a mere two hours. Is that, Nashe wondered, where we are heading in this country, too? Where every person fulfills his duty with the immediacy of a machine and not the thought, feeling, and judgment of a human being? Where panic, distrust, and betrayal replace whatever instincts may have survived in us of patience, courage, and trust?

CHAPTER 14

PAUL RICHTER WAS AN OLD friend of Nashe, though one he had not seen in years. He was born in Leipzig and studied art history in East Berlin, becoming curator of the Kupferstichkabinett at a young age and publishing articles on Italian and Flemish old masters. He was highly regarded in the art world.

Richter defected to the west around nineteen seventy-five, but no one knew exactly when or how. Nashe once asked him, but Richter merely frowned and said nothing, the moment passing in prolonged, awkward silence. Nashe never asked again.

What Nashe did know was that, before he met him, Richter had been in London for a number of years publishing articles and working as curator in the drawings department of the British Museum. He had become a leading connoisseur, one who specializes in the attribution of works of art to the artists who produced them.

Every so often an article will appear in the news about an artwork purchased for a small sum of money which later proves to be a priceless work by an old master. Such things do happen, but rarely. What is much more common, but almost never talked about, is the process happening in reverse: the successful re-attribution of a number of artworks from the most famous old masters to the lesser known artists who, it turns out, actually created them.

Richter once explained the process to Nashe this way: there was a centripetal force in the attribution of works of art during the eighteenth century when most of the major art collections were formed. Wealthy collectors were attracted to the great names — Rubens, Titian, Rembrandt, Bruegel — and they easily convinced themselves that an almost-Rubens was an absolute Rubens. Now, however, the force is centrifugal, with works previously attached to a few great names being spun out to a growing number of less celebrated artists.

One of the first bombs that Paul Richter dropped on the art world was the convincing, indeed apparently bullet-proof, reattribution of a well-known Titian drawing in the British Museum to one of Titian's students Domenico Campagnola. As Titian's drawings normally sell for hundreds of thousands of dollars, and Domenico Campagnola's maybe a twentieth of that, this was quite a financial blow for the museum to absorb.

But there was more to it than that. Museums live off the gifts of wealthy patrons. Sometimes these patrons donate works directly from their own private collections. Sometimes, they supply large sums of money for the purchase of particular works on the market. In either case, these patrons do not like to see any of their gifts reduced to a fraction of its value.

The trouble doesn't end there. Attributions stand like a pyramid upside down. When drawing A is attributed to, let's say, Van Dyke, and drawing B is shown to be by the same hand as A, then B is called a Van Dyke also. And then C is linked to B, and so on through a long chain of attributions all dependent on the original attribution of A. But what if A is convincingly shown to be the work of another, lesser artist? In that case all the attributions standing upon it fall together, and the combined loss of value may total millions of dollars to collections all over the world. This was the case with the British Museum Titian.

Things in the art world happen slowly and quietly. Paul Richter was next heard of as an art consultant in London, no longer employed by the British Museum. His importance as a scholar was indisputable, and when it gradually became known that he was indeed available, our own National Gallery made him an offer to head its drawings department. Negotiations went back and forth for several months, when finally Richter accepted and moved to this country. This was when Nashe came in contact with him through a mutual friend.

Paul Richter's method when the attribution of a work bothered him was to have the drawing placed on an easel on his desk so that he would have it constantly before him and could study it minutely during breaks from his other work. What he was looking for were the characteristic movements of the artist's hand as it passed over the sheet and left its marks upon it. Lines leading into the distance that broke up into dashes and then dots. Hatching and shading on figures or ground. The rapid, unthinking squiggles that indicated shrubbery or leaves on distant trees. It was in these unpremeditated and relatively insignificant details that an artist revealed his identity.

Almost the first thing Paul Richter did when he assumed his new post was ask to have a large, magnificent Bruegel landscape, one of the stars of the collection, placed on an easel on his desk. The first time Nashe was invited to Richter's office, he asked about it. "There's something wrong with that Bruegel," Richter said. "I'm not the only one to think so, but everyone says 'It's so great a drawing, only Bruegel could have done it.' That's a terribly weak argument. All this talk about major artists and minor artists. Even a minor artist will create a major work. It may only happen once in his life, but it happens."

A year later, Paul Richter published an article attributing the drawing to a contemporary of Bruegel named Roelandt Savery. The dominoes started falling one by one in museum collections around the world. The media picked up the story and questioned the expenditure of public money on works of art that may not even be authentic. Two influential board members attacked Richter's judgement, even though most scholars agreed with him. In the midst of all this commotion, Nashe called Richter and invited him for a drink.

"I don't know if I ever told you about the moped gangs," Richter said. "They've been much on my mind lately. After the war, and the division of Germany, there were many young men, teenagers, too young to have fought in the war, no jobs, no purpose in life, hanging around with nothing to do. They had seen the movies and wanted to be bikers like you have here, tough Hell's Angels. They could never afford Harley-Davidsons, so they formed gangs with their little mopeds — you know, motor-pedal bikes — and hung out in the public squares, and smoked and drank beer and raced around the streets causing a whole lot of trouble. It made them feel like they were something.

"The Russians had annexed all of eastern Europe, and your country was certain they were not done, that they would try to spread their system to the west. Germany was in tatters, of course. There was no way we could have resisted the Russians if they tried to expand, so your General Marshall came up with a plan to rebuild Germany, get its businesses going again, make it strong enough to stand against the communists.

"It wasn't easy, of course, to convince everyone. Your people said, Why should we rebuild the Nazi's after what we paid already to stop them? Marshall and Truman launched a giant propaganda campaign to prove that the Germans were now your friends, they were no longer Nazis.

"So, one day an agent — nobody knows whether he was a Russian agent or an East German agent — was walking around Munich when he noticed boys in a moped gang and started talking to them. He offered them fifty marks, about twenty dollars, to ride round at night and paint swastikas and "Death to Jews" on the front of Jewish businesses. You see, they had already started a program of rebuilding Jewish businesses for Jews who had chosen to stay.

"So, the boys did it, the press reported it, and the story spread round the world. And everyone said 'You see, the Germans are still Nazis, still anti-semites.' A week later, the agent paid the gang to do it again. That confirmed it in everybody's mind.

"Here in your country, this was a big problem. People were very upset. Why are we giving money to Nazis? Marshall and Truman poured millions of more dollars into propaganda. Congress had to reduce the program from fifteen billions to twelve billions. The Marshall Plan almost died. And why? All because a clever foreign agent had shown everybody the truth.

"You see, the Germans did not stop being anti-semites just because in nineteen forty-eight General Marshall said so. But your country wanted people to believe the lie. They were willing to spend millions of dollars to protect the lie, because the lie was more useful to them than the truth.

"I have been thinking about this lately, because people have been saying to me 'Why did you take away our beautiful Bruegel drawing?' They are angry with me. But I haven't taken it away. They still have it. And it is just as beautiful as it ever was. But now they have the truth, that it wasn't made by Bruegel, it was made by Savery. But they don't want the truth. They want the lie, because the lie is worth more money than the truth."

That was the last time Nashe saw his friend Paul Richter. At some point in the following weeks, Richter quietly packed up and disappeared. The next Nashe heard, Richter was in Frankfort, working as an art consultant. Nashe wrote him and received a letter in return. Richter seemed to be all right, but he was so private a man it was hard to tell for sure.

CHAPTER 15

BABY TANYA WAS A *cause celebre* thirty years ago. Nashe remembered following the story in the news. Galina Rovskya, a Russian translator and political analyst, claimed that her baby Tanya was the child of a diplomatic attaché named Michael Parry who had been posted to Moscow and was now back in this country. He admitted they had an affair. He claimed he knew nothing about the pregnancy. She requested visas for herself and her child to enter our country. Parry supported her request, but both her government and ours had objections.

Questions and theories abounded: Was she a spy who had compromised him? He claimed it was a purely romantic relationship, but a photograph of them at an embassy function did little to help his cause, at least in the court of public opinion. Rovskya, tall, beautiful, with a thick mane of blonde hair, was the very picture of the *femme fatale.* Parry was a head shorter, balding, and somewhat pudgy. The public wanted to know, Should Parry lose his job? Had our security interests been compromised? Had they plotted together and were now using the baby as a way for Rovskya to gain citizenship? Will the Russians let her go? Will they punish her if she stays? And *What*, the popular press demanded, *Will Become of Baby Tanya?* the headline blazoned above a photograph of the adorable infant.

Whatever the underlying truth of the matter, it was all sorted out rather sensibly. Our government granted the mother and child visas, and the Russians let them go. The parents would not marry, but they committed themselves to doing what was best for the girl. The father bought them a comfortable home, arranged private day care for the baby, and found Galina a job as a teacher of languages at a nearby college. He saw them almost every day and provided whatever support was needed.

And Tanya, whose actual name was Tatiana Mikhailovna Rovskya, grew up to be the kind of child every parent dreams of: tall, lovely, healthy, brilliant, and most of all gloriously happy, always with a big smile on her face. She excelled at everything because she loved everything. Latin in fifth grade? *How fun!* Calculus in tenth? *Fascinating!* She was enrolled in private schools, attended an elite college, and graduated from a top law school. She was hired by the agency, moved up quickly, and, within only a few short years, became the youngest director of the legal division in its history.

Nashe received a call from Ms Rovskya's secretary to ask if he was available for a meeting. "Could you come this morning at 10:00am?" she said, "Ms Rovskya would like to take care of this as quickly as possible."

Well, Nashe thought, it has finally happened. They wouldn't ask him to see the head of the legal division if they hadn't made some kind of important decision, most certainly a bad one for him. It was nine o'clock. Nashe collected his papers and locked them in his desk. If they were going to fire him, or prosecute him, or both, then he needn't do any work. He would sit and rest and think for an hour.

Nashe recalled his last conversation with Paul Richter, several years ago. Perhaps Richter was right: that people prefer the lie to the truth, and that even a single, small, isolated truth could forestall a great nation. But what was that truth? And was it even true? Nashe had no idea. He thought he had submitted an ordinary report, whatever that means, yet somehow he created a perfect storm of threat and panic, annoyance and disgust that he could not understand and could never have predicted.

But really, Nashe thought, it was inevitable that it should end this way. He had been drifting long enough in a job he no longer believed in, living a life that was a dodge and a lie. He'd known that for some time. And he should have guessed that, sooner or later, everyone around him would know it, too. Most likely they did, and it was possible they had even planned all this. They had made a decision for him that he should have made for himself long ago. Somehow, he had lost his way. And if it was time for him to leave, to start over, to try to recover the right path in his life, then he would go. What other choice did he have?

Nashe walked down several long corridors to the legal division, strangely aware of his surroundings, as he would not be seeing them again. When he arrived in the waiting room of Ms Rovskya's office, her secretary said, "Oh, Mr Nashe, you can go right in."

Nashe opened the door, stepped in, and closed it behind him. Ms Rovskya put down her papers, jumped up quickly, and walked around her desk to Nashe with her hand extended. She looked like her mother in a photograph Nashe remembered, but with darker hair.

"Mr Nashe, thank you for coming. I am *so* sorry!" She shook Nashe's hand and asked him to sit down. "I've been reviewing your case. Oh, my God! What you must have been going though!" She laughed a tinkly laugh, saying "I mean, it's just crazy!" She sat down and picked up a stack of papers.

"Of course the whole thing is going to be thrown out. I mean, just look at this." She read a bit and giggled. "How crazy! I mean, it was a public forum. There wasn't any classified information going around, and you didn't have any in your report. I've read the whole thing."

She picked up another sheet. "We asked for a counter-intel report. You weren't even exposed to classified information. It's just insane!" She read silently a bit more. "The leaks weren't based on your report. And wherever they did come from, they probably weren't even true."

Ms Rovskya turned to the brief again and read silently for a moment. Then she burst into her tinkly laugh.

"Treason! Ha ha ha!" She could barely control herself. "That's funny! I'm sorry. I shouldn't be laughing. But that's too much!"

After she'd collected herself, Ms Rovskya said, "Let me assure you, Mr Nashe, this case is closed. It shouldn't have been opened in the first place. I'm very, very sorry. This is not how we do things around here. At least, not normally. We have great lawyers — I mean, like, really, really smart people — but some of them have to learn to color inside the lines."

Ms Rovskya rose from her chair, walked around her desk, and led Nashe to the door. "So…" she said, "I am sorry. This won't happen again. I apologize if it caused you any worry, which I'm sure it did since this isn't a very nice process. So… I guess that's it! I'm so glad I got to meet you, Mr Nashe. Come and see me any time you have a question."

Ms Rovskya smiled happily, shook Nashe's hand, and said goodbye.

CHAPTER 16

ISHA GANDEKAR'S FAMILY HAD BEEN princes in Maharashtra, India since the eighteenth century, until their rule was dissolved by the new government in nineteen forty-eight. They were Deshastha Brahmins, the original Brahmins in their state, all other Brahmins falling below them in status.

Isha was studying at the university when she met Rajat Varne, also a Brahmin, but of a lower sub-caste, and from a family of relatively modest means. They fell in love. Rajat asked Isha's father for her hand in marriage and was immediately refused. Isha's family had exalted plans for their daughter. She was, after all, by birth, if not by title, a princess.

Isha's mother quickly set about finding a suitable match for her daughter. Dinner parties were arranged to which were invited several eligible young men and their families. After each party, her mother asked which of the young men should be invited again. Each time, Isha answered "None of them."

After several months of invitations and dinners, Isha's mother decided on a different tactic. She enlisted Isha's four aunts and three married cousins, and together they assaulted Isha with all the arguments they could muster. His family has no connections, they would say. Who will socialize with you? Nobody we know. And think how selfish you are being! If you marry this man, you will be degrading your entire family. Think how you are hurting the chances of your sister and your younger cousins. All of their marriage prospects will fall because of you!

Isha fought back as best she could. Rajat is a Brahmin, she said, just like us all. Who cares if he is not as exalted as we are? And Rajat has a degree in business, he wants to work in a bank. We will make our own way.

Isha's aunts mounted a counter offensive. Nobody cares if this man wants to become a clerk in some bank. What kind of job is that? Anyway, men who marry into our family become part of the family business. (They retained vast holdings of land, with substantial income from mining and agriculture.) A stupid girl like you should not even be thinking about money! You should be thinking about your duty and your family and your reputation in the world!

Somewhere in the midst of this tirade, Isha fell into a kind of trance. The scolding voices faded away. Her aunts and cousins disappeared from sight. All that remained was a vision of Rajat. He was smiling and speaking to her. Isha thought to herself: This is the most brilliant and most beautiful man I have ever seen.

When Isha snapped out of her vision, she stood up and proclaimed, "Rajat Varne is the man I love, and he is the only man in the world I will marry," and walked out.

In olden times, Isha might have been locked into a room to starve until she saw reason. Fortunately, her father was not so unreasonable. He told her that she and Rajat must wait a year. If Rajat's career prospered and it was clear that he would be able to support her, then he would give his consent.

Rajat Varne was hardly a bank clerk. He had been a top student at the university, earning a degree in finance with a specialization in international markets and mathematical modeling. He was offered positions with several investment banks in Mumbai, choosing to go with a foreign firm because they paid more, and, in Rajat's experience, knew little and cared less about India's complex caste system.

Rajat did exceptionally well at the bank, to say the least. Within a short time, he was promoted to chief investment strategist for Asian markets. The firm's assets under management, once counted in B's for billions were soon over a T for trillion. Rajat and Isha were married with her father's blessing, and, not long after, the firm offered Rajat promotion to their headquarters in this country.

Rajat and Isha thought seriously about the move. Against it was leaving their families and friends. For it was a much higher salary, and, at long last, a social field in which they could start afresh, free from the confines of caste. They were still debating this decision when Isha discovered that she was pregnant. They chose to wait for the baby to be born before they accepted or declined the offer.

If Isha Varne had any doubts about marrying her husband (which she never had) those doubts would have been completely swept aside by the birth of her son, whom they named Arav. He was the most beautiful baby she had ever seen.

Then a curious thing happened. At almost the precise moment that Arav Varne entered the world, anti-Brahmin feeling in India, always present in one form or another, suddenly burst into prominence, especially in the universities. From there, the movement spread rapidly through the government, and then to business. A system of quotas was quickly established to favor non-Brahmins applying to university and graduates applying for jobs. The new policy was so prejudicial that thousands of Brahmins emigrated, the vast majority coming to this country. Rajat and Isha, considering their son's future, thought "Why should we stay in India, if Arav will not have a fair chance?" Their son had just reached two years of age when Rajat accepted his new position.

Growing up in this country, Arav Varne was a veritable prince on Earth. He was given the finest education, wore the best clothes, lived in the grandest homes, and took the most thrilling and elaborate of vacations. Like his parents, he was remarkably handsome. Also like them, he had impeccable manners and great charm. Most of all, Arav was sincere, and hard working, and tremendously intelligent.

The agency hired him straight out of college, and, like Mireille Jemmot before him, whom Varne followed as head of the division, he was universally recognized as someone destined for higher things.

Arav Varne appeared unexpectedly at Nashe's office an hour after Nashe's meeting with Tatiana Rovskya. As usual, he was immaculately dressed. He politely introduced himself (even though Nashe knew who he was), apologized for the way Nashe's case had been handled, and assured Nashe that this was no reflection on his work for the agency.

"I can see that you have been unfairly treated," Arav Varne said. "I have read your report, and I think I understand what you are trying to do. You present the facts insofar as you know them, then you stop short of drawing a conclusion. That is an interesting heuristic. You operate on the principle that free inquiry amongst ourselves, charged as we are with making decisions, is the best way to establish forward-looking solutions. I agree with that.

"I believe you have been facing resistance because many people find a lack of assertion unsettling. They interpret it as a lack of conviction, and lack of conviction they interpret as active opposition, which of course it is not.

"Our staff, as you know, come from all over the world, with different experiences and different backgrounds. But all of them are privileged to be here, working in this agency, where they have the opportunity to use their minds and training to make great changes in the world. But with that privilege comes a great deal of responsibility — an obligation to put aside biases and prejudices and to make decisions based on evidence and reason — to make absolutely certain that the facts really are the facts, to dig down deep and question their sources, and, even more than that, to question themselves, their motives and preconceptions, before they dare to establish what they think is the truth. Only then can they make decisions that could in any way be morally justifiable in the world.

"The interesting thing, which I admire a lot, is the way you have embodied that process in your report. It is too bad that it has been taken so erroneously, as though you were advancing a dangerous and heretical end product rather than providing an appropriate and useful exercise in consensus formation. That is a shame, since we need more of it.

"Anyway, I came here to tell you that I appreciate what you are doing, and to apologize for the trouble you have been through. That is not how I imagine the conduct of the division under my guidance."

CHAPTER 17

When Paul Richter worked at the National Gallery he curated a major loan exhibition of the prints and drawings of Albrecht Dürer. The museum's own holdings were bolstered with works borrowed from Frankfort, Vienna, Munich, and East Berlin. Richter and his staff designed the exhibition and wrote the catalogue. Two or three days before the opening, curators from the donating institutions hand-carried the selected works on commercial flights. Guards in plain clothes met them at the airport and escorted them to the Gallery. The curators were then put up in luxury hotels, all expenses paid, and were free to roam the city until the day of the opening when there would be a dinner, a lecture, and a press reception. The Städel Museum in Frankfort sent one curator, the Albertina in Vienna also one, the Alte Pinakothek in Munich two, and the Kupferstichkabinett in East Berlin a party of five: three curators accompanied by two unnamed men whom everyone knew were officers of the Stasi, the East German secret police.

The lecture was given by the head curator of the Alte Pinakothek. His subject was Dürer's print *Melencholia I.* The curator began by stating that although some scholars consider the print difficult to interpret, there is really no mystery to it at all. What do we see? Two angels sitting before a tower looking depressed and inert. Spread around them are tools of various human arts and sciences: a crucible in which man has tried to transmute the elements of nature, a compass for charting and mapping the earth, a sundial and hourglass for the measurement of time, a balance for weight, a sphere and a polyhedron for geometry, an inkwell for writing, and a "magic square" for mathematics. All ignored and neglected.

At the feet of the angels rests a hunting dog, a symbol of rational thought, since a dog follows the scent of his prey as the mind pursues truth, constantly searching back and forth, losing the track, finding it again, overshooting the mark, returning to where it started, never moving in a straight line, never flagging, and never giving up. But not this dog: rather, he is starved, neglected, asleep.

Bellow the angels, literally under their feet, symbols of Christ and his sacrifice: the saw and plane of his trade as a carpenter, the four nails from his crucifixion, even the pincers used to pull the nails out when he was taken down from the cross. All lie on the floor discarded like so much litter.

To the left of the angels, a censer, now extinguished, the source from which smoke rises to heaven to guide our thoughts and prayers. Beyond that, a rainbow and a comet streaking across the sky, signals from heaven that we are not alone.

Behind and slightly above the angels, a ladder which disappears beyond the top edge of the frame, and next to the ladder a bell attached to a rope, which also leads out of the frame, ready at any moment to be rung by unknown hands announcing…well, what? Only bat-like thoughts twitter in the background, fleeting, grotesque, and dark.

The angels do not sense the wonders around them, nor do they recognize the incomparable gifts they have been given. The small angel grinds on, working without hope; the other stares into the unknown, perceiving only darkness and emptiness without and within.

We feel a spiritual deadness here, a fear of reaching beyond oneself, a fear of setting out. The sea is empty, the ladder unclimbed, the signs from heaven unheeded, the sacrifice denied. The angels, given wings to fly, remain depressed, dispirited, and fixed upon the ground.

There is much to fear in this attitude. It is a sign of disturbance and violence to come. We feel that these frustrated inward desires must soon explode upon the world. The question we confront is that if angels can be stricken with this spiritual disease, angels who have seen God face to face, then what hope is there for us?

Scholars over the years have interpreted this picture in their own terms, but not in the terms of Albrecht Dürer. They take the print as a document of Humanism, and then of those off-shoots of Humanism: Modernism and Existentialism. But Dürer chose to show us not humans, but angels. To understand Dürer's allegory we must understand how, from his point of view, angels and humankind are connected. Remember, it was a hundred years after Dürer's death that southern German cities would burn thousands of witches every year. These people believed in spiritual beings, angels and demons, and they believed in spiritual possession — even the victims themselves believed it. Today, we do not believe, yet we continue to persecute and destroy millions of our fellow men and women all around the globe. How do we explain that? I am not suggesting that demons or angels walk among us now, but Dürer's picture tells us this: that before we pretend to understand anything about the world, we must first come to understand ourselves.

The lecture ended there. Nashe filed out of the auditorium with the other guests and started down the stairs to the exhibition. On the first landing he was met by Cara, Paul Richter's curatorial assistant, a woman in her early twenties. She took Nashe by the arm and whispered "Can I talk to you?" and led him into the office. He could feel that she was trembling.

"I think I've done a terrible thing," Cara said. "You know those East German curators — they never go anywhere. Every day they sit and do research in the Print Room, watched by those guards. So today I was in the stacks finding one of them a book, and he asked me very quietly if would I mail a letter for him. I thought maybe he doesn't know how to find the post office, or what our mailboxes look like. So I took his letter and mailed it after work. When I came back for the dinner, I was surprised to see they were still in the Print Room. So I said Josef, I mailed that letter for you. Josef jumped in his seat like he'd been slapped. The two security men turned and looked at him and surrounded him. And Josef just sat there frozen like....he ...he..." Nashe saw there were tears welling in her eyes. *"Oh, God! He looked so sad and so scared!"* Cara began to cry, short painful sobs. Nashe put his hand on Cara's shoulder and told her it was all right, it probably wouldn't mean anything.

"I panicked and ran out of the room...*Why am I so stupid?*...They must have taken him away...He wasn't at the dinner...I looked... *Do you think he thinks I did it on purpose?* ... Please don't tell Paul. *Please, Please*...Oh, God!... *What have I done?"* Cara covered her face with her hands and broke down sobbing.

Nashe said they should go, he would walk her home. Along the way, he tried to cheer her up. He told her nobody would think it was her fault. Anyone coming from those countries knows we don't understand these things. And they probably won't do anything to him anyway. That was just the old days. They don't throw people in jail just for writing a letter. They're much more open now. Nashe kept talking, on and on. It was all lies and he knew it, but Cara was so crushed and miserable that he had to say something.

It was a month before Nashe returned to the Gallery. When he did, Cara pulled him aside and said, "I have to tell you something. I made a follow-up call to East Berlin about the the drawings. When I was done — I couldn't help myself — I said I'd like to speak to Dr. Josef Beckmann, please — he was the curator. There was a pause on the other end. I thought the line had gone dead, so I said, Are you there? Yes, the woman said. So I said, I'd like to speak to Dr. Josef Beckmann. There was another long pause. Finally the woman said, rather irritated, I'm sorry, Miss, but no such person works at this museum." Cara stopped speaking and stared at the floor for a long time. Nashe thought she was going to cry, but she held it back. Then Cara looked up, drew a deep breath, and in a trembling voice said, "I'll never forget the look he gave me. That poor man! He was so terrified. And I did that. I don't think I'll ever forgive myself."

CHAPTER 18

He would be late, as unexpected meetings with Rovskya and Varne had put him behind in his work. When Nashe finally looked up from his desk, the sky was dark outside his window. The corridors were empty. He was the only one on the floor.

Nashe sat back and reflected on all that had happened to him. In spite of the assurances he had been given, Nashe did not believe that the problem had been laid to rest. An explosion of such violence and irrationality always produces unexpected and often more dangerous aftershocks. No, Nashe had merely scratched the surface of something deeper, something smoldering in the depths, some rage or fury waiting to be unleashed that would certainly erupt again.

Nashe's mind went back to that East German curator, the cold chill of that moment, the one unforgivable error that a lifetime of care and watchfulness could never retract, and how Nashe had naively believed that such things could not happen here. These last few days had undeceived him. Nashe reflected on the horror that such things happen at all, and the cowardice and narrowness of mind of those who must persecute and destroy any who disagree with them, the fanaticism and hatred needed to drive people to that extreme, how it becomes a sickness and mania that spreads within a society and which no one has the strength or courage to resist.

Nashe gathered the papers on his desk and closed the document on his computer. It would not save. He tried again. Again, it would not save. He tried a third time. No luck. He thought, maybe I can save it in a different program. He couldn't. Maybe I can revert the document to an earlier version. It wouldn't do that either. Nashe opened a directory, scrolled back into his history, opened a document at random and tried to save that. It wouldn't save. This was a problem.

Nashe paused a moment to consider what to do next. While he did so, his eye fell inevitably to the newly opened document. His own words and ideas now seemed completely alien to him. Had he actually written it? He noticed there were several earlier documents in the thread. Perhaps one of those might reveal to Nashe what he had been thinking when he had created this document. But how would Nashe explain why he had been thinking *that*? Would he have to find a still earlier document, and then one before that, and one before that, stretching in a long chain back to before there were documents, before there was speech, before he even knew what words were? Where was Nashe to find a valid basis for his judgment on matters that he now came to realize he understood not at all?

Nashe looked at the time. It was growing quite late. He debated with himself for a moment, then moved his finger over the power button. When Nashe pressed that button and crashed his computer he would very probably lose all of the work he had completed that day. But it had to be done. He wasn't planning to be here forever.

Nashe pressed the button. Sooner than he expected, a message flashed across the screen:

FATAL ERROR! BRING COMPUTER TO COMPUTER CENTER IMMEDIATELY!

Nashe rose from his desk, collected his things, locked his office door, and walked along the corridor to its end. The computer center was in the second sub-basement, a secure location three floors below street level. At the bottom of the staircase, Nashe found a locked door which he opened with a key card. This led to another long corridor which ended at another locked door. Nashe used his key card again.

The room Nashe entered was a concrete cell, with a mirrored window on the wall opposite the door, and a single drawer below the window. On the left near the ceiling was a box attached to the wall containing a camera. In the center of the room was a table with a microphone and a chair. Nashe sat down and, speaking into the microphone, said he had received a message to bring his computer here. There was no response. The center was supposed to be staffed twenty four hours a day, all days of the year. Maybe someone was just taking a break. Nashe tried again; again he received no response.

Nashe opened his computer. The screen now showed three directories side by side with files scrolling up from the bottom and disappearing at the top. Everything in his computer was being erased, starting from the present and driving inexorably into the past. Two years were gone, then four, then six. Then, gradually, the procession started to slow down, like a roulette wheel coming to rest. A document entitled "Resignation" drifted to the top of the directory on the left and stopped there. Nashe opened it. Apparently, he had written the letter many years ago but never sent it. Reading it over, Nashe thought he could have written it today. Simple and direct, the letter said no more and no less than it had to: a decision had been made, there was no one to blame, and nothing to regret.

Nashe looked at the other directories. The computer's programs were being uninstalled one by one; his contacts were disappearing, with the sole exception of Deputy Director, which was stationed unmoving at the top. The Deputy Director, it occurred to Nashe, was in charge of hiring and firing. Okay, Nashe said to himself, I get it now. I see what's happening. Nashe felt a sudden twinge of fear, but not too much.

Nashe clicked on Deputy Director, created an email, attached his resignation letter to it, and then pressed send. He watched closely. After a brief delay, the screen on Nashe's computer turned completely blue except for a few indecipherable lines of code in white. Nashe had heard of this screen but had never seen it. It was called the Screen of Death. His computer no longer responded to his commands.

Nashe sat and reflected for a moment, but reflected on nothing. Then Nashe quickly stood up, stepped around the table, touched the lock with the key, and opened the drawer on the wall. Into the drawer, Nashe placed his computer, his ID, and his key card. Then Nashe slid the drawer closed and heard it lock.

Nashe exited the room, walked to the end of the corridor, and climbed the first two flights of stairs towards a side exit he knew about. Nashe, who had been wandering these halls for a quarter of a century, realized that from this point on he would have to find a new way of ordering his experience, a new way of giving purpose and direction to his life beyond working, and eating, and sleeping.

Nashe soon reached the foot of the final staircase that would take him back to the world. He was slightly winded and paused a moment to catch his breath. He knew there was no turning back. He was all right with that.

Nashe began to climb again, reached the top of the stairs, and pushed open the final door. He felt a chill on his face and could hear the banners flapping gently in the breeze. Nashe slowly looked around, then gazed up, and, breathing deep the cool night air, stepped out once more under the stars.

Made in the USA
Middletown, DE
20 June 2021

42051088R10083